Told in a French Garden

Mildred Aldrich

Contents

TOLD IN A FRENCH GARDEN

BY

Mildred Aldrich

INTRODUCTION
HOW WE CAME INTO THE GARDEN

It was by a strange irony of Fate that we found ourselves reunited for a summer's outing, in a French garden, in July, 1914.

With the exception of the Youngster, we had hardly met since the days of our youth.

We were a party of unattached people, six men, two women, your humble servant, and the Youngster, who was an outsider.

With the exception of the latter, we had all gone to school or college or dancing class together, and kept up a sort of superficial acquaintance ever since--that sort of relation in which people know something of one another's opinions and absolutely nothing of one another's real lives.

There was the Doctor, who had studied long in Germany, and become an authority on mental diseases, developed a distaste for therapeutics, and a passion for research and the laboratory. There was the Lawyer, who knew international law as he knew his Greek alphabet, and hated a court room. There was the Violinist, who was known the world over in musical sets,--everywhere, except in the concert room. There was the Journalist, who had travelled into almost as many queer places as Richard Burton, seen more wars, and followed more callings. There was the Sculptor, the fame of whose greater father had almost paralyzed a pair of good modeller's hands. There was the Critic, whose friends believed that in him the world had lost a great romancer, but whom a combination of hunger and laziness, and a proneness to think that nothing not genius was worth while, had condemned to be a mere breadwinner, but a breadwinner who squeezed a lot out of life, and who fervently believed that in his next incarnation he would really be "it." Then there was "Me," and of the other two women--one was a Trained Nurse, and the other a Divorcee, and--well, none of us really knew just what she had become, but we knew that she was very rich, and very handsome, and had a leaning toward some sort of new religion. As for the Youngster--he was the son of an old chum of the Doctor--his ward, in fact--and his hobby was flying.

Our reunion, after so many years, was a rather pretty story.

In the summer of 1913, the Doctor and the Divorcee, who had lost sight of one another for twenty years, met by chance in Paris. Her ex-husband had been a college friend of the Doctor. They saw a great deal of one another in the lazy way that people who really love France, and are done sightseeing, can do.

One day it occurred to them to take a day's trip into the country, as unattached people now and then can do. They might have gone out in a car--but they chose the railroad, with a walk at the end--on the principle that no one can know and love a country who does not press its earth beneath his feet,--the Doctor would probably have said, "lay his head upon its bosom." By an accident--they missed a train--they found themselves at sunset of a beautiful day in a small village, and with no possible way of getting back to Paris that night unless they chose to walk fifteen miles to the nearest railway junction. After a long day's tramp that seemed too much of a good thing.

So they looked about to find a shelter for the night. The village--it was only a hamlet--had no hotel, no cafe, even. Finally an old peasant said that old Mother Servin--a widow--living a mile up the road--had a big house, lived alone, and could take them in,--if she wanted to,--he could not say that she would.

It seemed to them worth trying, so they started off in high spirits to tramp another mile, deciding that, if worse became worst--well--the night was warm--they could sleep by the roadside under the stars.

It was near the hour when it should have been dark--but in France at that season one can almost read out of doors until nine--when they found the place. With some delay the gate in the stone wall was opened, and they were face to face with the old widow.

It was a long argument, but the Doctor had a winning way, and at the end they were taken in,--more, they were fed in the big clean kitchen, and then each was sheltered in a huge room, with cement floor, scrupulously clean, with the quaint old furniture and the queer appointments of a French farmhouse.

The next morning, when the Doctor threw open the heavy wooden shutters to his window, he gave a whistle of delight to find himself looking out into what seemed to be a French Paradise--and better than that he had never asked.

It was a wilderness. Way off in the distance he got glimpses of broken walls with all kinds of green things creeping and climbing, and hanging on for life. Inside the walls there was a riot of flowers--hollyhocks and giroflees, dahlias and phlox, poppies and huge daisies, and roses everywhere, even climbing old tree trunks, and sprawling all over the garden front of the rambling house. The edges of the paths had green borders that told of Corbeil d'Argent in Midwinter, and violets in early spring. He leaned out and looked along the house. It was just a jumble of all sorts of buildings which had evidently been added at different times. It seemed to be on half a dozen elevations, and no two windows were of the same size, while here and there an outside staircase led up into a loft.

Once he had taken it in he dressed like a flash--he could not get out into that garden quickly enough, to pray the Widow to serve coffee under a huge tree in the centre of the garden, about the trunk of which a rude table had been built, and it was there that the Divorcee found him when she came out, simply glowing with enthusiasm--the house, the garden, the Widow, the day--everything was perfect.

While they were taking their coffee, poured from the earthen jug, in the thick old Rouen cups, the Divorcee said:

"How I'd love to own a place like this. No one would ever dream of building such a house. It has taken centuries of accumulated needs to expand it into being. If one tried to do the thing all at once it would look too on-purpose. This place looks like a happy combination of circumstances which could not help itself."

"Well, why not? It might be possible to have just this. Let's ask the Widow."

So, when they were sitting over their cigarettes, and the old woman was clearing the table, the Doctor looked her over, and considered the road of approach.

She was a rugged old woman, well on toward eighty, with a bronzed, weather-worn face, abundant coarse gray hair, a heavy shapeless figure, but a firm bearing, in spite of her rounded back. As far as they could see, they were alone on the place with her. The Doctor decided to jump right into the subject.

"Mother," he said, "I suppose you don't want to sell this place?"

The old woman eyed him a moment with her sharp dark eyes.

"But, yes, ***Monsieur***," she replied. "I should like it very well, only it is not possible. No one would be willing to pay my price. Oh, no, no one. No, indeed."

"Well," said the Doctor, "how do you know that? What is the price?--Is it permitted to ask?"

The old woman hesitated,--started to speak--changed her mind, and turned away, muttering. "Oh, no, ***Monsieur***,--it is not worth the trouble--no one will ever pay my price."

The Doctor jumped up, laughing, ran after her, took her by the arm, and led her back to the table.

"Now, come, come, Mother," he remarked, "let us hear the price at any rate. I am so curious."

"Well," said the Widow, "it is like this. I would like to get for it what my brother paid for it, when he bought it at the death of my father--it was to settle with the rest of the heirs--we were eight then. They are all dead but me. But no, no one will ever pay that price, so I may as well let it go to my niece. She is the last. She doesn't need it. She has land enough. The cultivator has a hard time these days. It is as much as I can do to make the old place feed me and pay the taxes, and I am getting old. But no one will ever pay the price, and what will my brother think of me when the ***bon Dieu*** calls me, if I sell it for less than he paid? As for that, I don't know what he'll say to me for selling it at all. But I am getting old to live here alone--all alone. But no one will ever pay the price. So I may as well die here, and then my brother can't blame me. But it is lonely now, and I am growing too old. Besides, I don't suppose ***you*** want to buy it. What would a gentleman do with this?"

"Well," said the Doctor, "I don't really know what a ***gentleman would*** do with it," and he added, under his breath, in English, "but I know mighty well what this fellow ***could*** do with it, if he could get it," and he lighted a fresh cigarette.

The keen old eyes had watched his face.

"I don't suppose ***you*** want to buy it?" she persisted.

"Well," responded the Doctor, "how can a poor man like me say, if you don't care to name your price, and unless that price is within reason?"

After some minutes of hesitation the old woman drew a deep breath. "Well," she said, with the determination of one who expected to be scoffed at, "I won't take a ***sou*** less than my brother paid."

"Come on, Mother," said the Doctor, "what *did* your brother pay? No nonsense, you know."

"Well, if you must know--it was FIVE THOUSAND FRANCS, and I can't and won't sell it for less. There, now!"

There was a long silence.

The Doctor and his companion avoided one another's eyes. After a while, he said in an undertone, in English: "By Jove, I'm going to buy it."

"No, no," remonstrated his companion, her eyes gazing down the garden vista to where the wistaria and clematis and flaming trumpet flower flaunted on the old wall. "I am going to have it--I thought of it first. I want it."

"So do I," laughed the Doctor. "Never wanted anything more in all my life."

"For how long," she asked, "would a rover like you want this?"

"Rover yourself! And you? Besides what difference does it make how *long* I want it--since I want it *now*? I want to give a party--haven't given a party since-- since Class Day."

The Divorcee sighed. Still gazing down the garden she said quietly: "How well I remember--ninety-two!"

Then there was another silence before she turned to him suddenly: "See here- -all this is very irregular-so, that being the case--why shouldn't we buy it together? We know each other. Neither of us will ever stay here long. One summer apiece will satisfy us, though it is lovely. Be a sport. We'll draw lots as to who is to have the first party."

The Doctor waved the old woman away. Her keen eyes watched too sharply. Then, with their elbows on the table, they had a long and heated argument. Probably there were more things touched on than the garden. Who knows? At the end of it the Divorcee walked away down that garden vista, and the old woman was called and the Doctor took her at her word. And out of that arrangement emerged the scheme which resulted in our finding ourselves, a year later, within the old walls of that French garden.

Of course a year's work had been done on the interior, and Doctor and Divorcee had scoured the department for old furniture. Water had been brought a great distance, a garage had been built with servants' quarters over it--there were no servants in the house,--but the look of the place, we were assured, had not been changed, and both Doctor and Divorcee declared that they had had the year of their lives. Well, if they had, the place showed it.

But, as Fate would have it, the second night we sat down to dinner in that garden, news had come of the assassination of Franz Ferdinand-Charles-Louis Joseph-Marie d'Autriche-Este, whom the tragic death of Prince Rudolphe, almost exactly twenty-four years and six months earlier to a day, had made Crown Prince of Austria-Hungary--and the tone of our gathering was changed. From that day the party threatened to become a little Bedlam, and the garden a rostrum.

In the earlier days it did not make so much difference. The talk was good. We were a travelled group, and what with reminiscences of people and places, and the scandal of courts, it was far from being dull. But as the days went on, and the war clouds began to gather, the overcharged air seemed to get on the nerves of the entire group, and instead of the peaceful summer we had counted upon, every one of us seemed to live in his own particular kind of fever. Every one of us, down to the Youngster, had fixed ideas, deep-set theories, and convictions as different as our characters, our lives, our callings, and our faiths. We were all Cosmopolitan Americans, but ready to spread the Eagle, if necessary, and all of us, except the Violinist, of New England extraction, which means really of English blood, and that *will* show when the screws are put on. We had never thought of the Violinist as not one of us, but he was really of Polish origin. His great-grandfather had been a companion of Adam Czartoriski in the uprising of 1830, and had gone to the States when the amnesty was not extended to his chief after that rebellion, Poland's last, had been stamped out.

As well as I can remember it was the night of August 6th that the first serious dispute arose. England had declared war. All our male servants had left us except two American chauffeurs, and a couple of old outside men. Two of our four cars, and all our horses but one had been requisitioned. That did not upset us. We had taken on the wives of some of the men, among them Angele, the pretty wife of one of the French chauffeurs, and her two-months-old baby into the bargain. We still had two cars, that, at a pinch, would carry the party, and we still had one mount in case of necessity.

The question arose as to whether we should break up and make for the nearest port while we could, or "stick it out." It had been finally agreed not to evacuate--yet. One does not often get such a chance to see a country at war, and we were all ardent spectators, and all unattached. I imagine not one of us had at that time any idea of being useful--the stupendousness of it all had not dawned on any of us--unless it was the Doctor.

But after the decision of "stick" had been passed unanimously, the Critic, who was a bit of a sentimentalist, and if he were anything else was a Norman Angel-lite, stuck his hands in his pockets, and remarked: "After all, it is perfectly safe to stay, especially now that England is coming in."

"You think so?" said the Doctor.

"Sure," smiled the Critic. "The Germans will never cross the French frontier this time. This is not 1870."

"Won't they, and isn't it?" replied the Doctor sharply.

"They never can get by Verdun and Belfort."

"Never said they could," remarked the Doctor, with a tone as near to a sneer as a good-natured host can allow himself. "But they'll invade fast enough. I know what I am talking about."

"You don't mean to tell me," said the Critic, "that a nation like Germany--I'm talking now about the people, the country that has been the hot bed of Socialism,--will stand for a war of invasion?"

That started the Doctor off. He flayed the theorists, the people who reasoned with their emotions and not their brains, the mob that looked at externals, and never saw the fires beneath, the throng that was unable to understand anything outside its own horizon, the mass that pretended to read the history of the world, and because it changed its clothes imagined that it had changed its spirit.

"Why, I've lived in Germany," he cried. "I was educated there. I know them. I have the misfortune to understand them. They'll stick together and Socialism go hang--as long as there is a hope of victory. The Confederation was cemented in the blood of victory. It can only be dissolved in the blood of defeat. They are a great, a well-disciplined, and an obedient people."

"One would think you admired them and their military system," remarked the Critic, a bit crest-fallen at the attack.

"I may not, but I'll tell you one sure thing if you want a good circus you've got to train your animals. The Kaiser has been a corking ringmaster."

Of course this got a laugh, and though both Critic and Journalist tried to strike fire again with words like "democracy" and "civilization," the Doctor had cooled down, and nothing could stir him again that night.

Still the discord had been sown. I suppose the dinner-table talk was only a sample of what was going on, in that month, all over the world. It did not help matters that as the days went on we all realized that the Doctor had been right--that France was to be invaded, not across her own proper frontier, but across unprotected Belgium. This seemed so atrocious to most of us that indignation could only express itself in abuse. There was not a night that the dinner-table talk was not bitter. You see the Doctor did not expect the world ever to be perfect--did not know that he wanted it to be--believed in the struggle. On the other hand the Critic, and in a certain sense the Journalist, in spite of their experiences, were more or less Utopian, and the Sculptor and the Violinist purely spectators.

No need to go into the details of the heated arguments. They were only the echo of what all the world,--that had cradled itself into the belief that a great war among the great nations had become, for economic as well as humanitarian reasons, impossible,--were, I imagine, at this time saying.

As nearly as I can remember it was on August 20th that the climax came. Liege had fallen. The English Expedition had landed, and was marching on Belgium. A victorious German army had goose-stepped into defenseless Brussels, and was sweeping out toward the French frontier. The French advance into Alsace had been a blunder.

The Doctor remarked that "the English had landed twelve days too late," and the Journalist drew a graphic, and purely imaginary, picture of the pathos of the Belgians straining their eyes in vain to the West for the coming of the men in khaki, and unfortunately he let himself expatiate a bit on German methods.

The spark touched the Doctor off.

"By Jove," he said, "all you sentimentalists read the History of the World with your intellects in your breeches pockets. War is not a game for babies. It is war--it is not sport. You chaps think war can be prevented. All I ask you is--why hasn't it been prevented? In every generation that we know anything about there have been some pretty fine men who have been of your opinion--Erasmus for one, and how many others? But since the generations have contented themselves with talking, and not talked war out of the problem, why, I can't see, for my part, that Germany's way is not as good as any. She is in to win, and so are all the rest of them. Schools of War are like the Schools of Art you chaps talk so much about--it does not make much difference what school one belongs to--the only important thing is making good."

"One would think," said the Journalist, "that you *liked* such a war."

"Well, I don't even know that I can deny that. I would not deliberately *choose* it. But I am willing to accept it, and I am not a bit sentimental about it. I am not even sure that it was not needed. The world has let the Kaiser sit twenty-five years on a throne announcing himself as 'God's anointed.' His pretensions have been treated seriously by all the democracies of the world. What for? Purely for personal gain. We have come to a pass where there is little a man won't do--for personal gain. The business of the world, and its diplomacy, have all become so complicated and corrupt that a large percentage of the brains of honest mankind are little willing to touch either. We need shaking up--all of us. If nothing can make man realize that he was not born to be merely happy and get rich, or to have a fine old time, why, such a complete upheaval as this seems to me to be necessary, and for me--if this war can rip off, with its shrapnel, the selfishness with which prosperity has encrusted the lucky: if it can explode our false values with its bombs: if it can break down our absurd pretensions with its cannon,--all I can say is that Germany will have done missionary work for the whole world--herself included."

Before he had done, we were all on our feet shouting at him, all but the Lawyer, who smiled into his coffee cup.

"Why," cried the Critic, in anger, "one would think you held a brief for them!"

"I do NOT," snapped the Doctor, "but I don't dislike them any more than I do--well," catching himself up with a laugh, "lots of other people."

"And you mean to tell me," said the gentle voice of the Divorcee at his elbow, "that you calmly face the idea of the hundreds of thousands of men,--well and strong to-day--dead to-morrow,--the thought of the mothers who have borne their sons in pain, and bred them in love, only to fling them before the cannon?"

"For what, after all, *are* we born?" said the Doctor. "Where we die, or *when* is a trifle, since die we must. But *why* we die and *how* is vital. It is not only vital to the man that goes--it is vital to the race. It is the struggle, it is the fight, which, no matter what form it takes, makes life worth living. Men struggle for money. Financiers strangle one another at the Bourse. People look on and applaud, in spite of themselves. That is exciting. It is not uplifting. But for men just like you and me to march out to face death for an idea, for honor, for duty, that very fact ennobles the race."

"Ah," said the Lawyer, "I see. The Doctor enjoys the drama of life, but he does not enjoy the purely domestic drama."

"And out of all this," said the Trained Nurse, in her level voice, "you are leaving the Almighty. He gave us a world full of beauty, full of work, full of interest, and he gave us capacities to enjoy it, and endowed us with emotions which make it worth while to live and to die. He gave us simple laws--they are clear enough--they mark sharply the line between good and evil. He left us absolutely free to choose. And behold what man has made of it!"

"I deny the statement," said the Doctor.

"That's easy," laughed the Journalist.

"I believe," said the Doctor, impatiently, "that no good comes but through evil. Read your Bible."

"I don't want to read it with *your* eyes," replied the Journalist, and marched testily down the path toward the house.

"Well," snapped the Doctor, "if I read it with *yours*, I should call on the Almighty to smite this planet with his fires and send us spinning, a flaming brand through space, to annihilation--the great scheme would seem to me a failure--but I don't believe it is." And off he marched in the other direction.

The Lawyer shrugged his shoulders, and suppressed, as well as he could, a smile. The Youngster, leaning his elbows on his knees, recited under his breath:

"And as he sat, all suddenly there rolled,   From where the woman wept upon the sod,   Satan's deep voice, 'Oh Thou unhappy God.'"

"Exactly," said the Lawyer.

"What's that?" asked the Violinist.

"Only the last three lines of a great little poem by a little great Irishman named Stephens--entitled 'What Satan Said.'"

"After all," said the Lawyer, "the Doctor is probably right. It all depends on one's point of view."

"And one's temperament," said the Violinist.

"And one's education," said the Critic.

Just here the Doctor came back,--and he came back his smiling self. He made a dash down the path to where the Journalist was evidently sulking, went up behind him, threw an arm over his shoulder, and led him back into the circle.

"See here," he said, "you are all my guests. I am unreasonably fond of you, even if we can't see Life from the same point of view. Man as an individual, and Man as a part of the Scheme are two different things. I asked you down here to enjoy yourselves, not to argue. I apologize--all my fault--unpardonable of me. Come now--we have decided to stay as long as we can--we are all interested. It is not every generation that has the honor to sit by, and watch two systems meet at the crossroads and dispute the passage to the Future. We'll agree not to discuss the ethics of the matter again. If the men marching out there to the frontier can agree to face the cannon-- and there are as many opinions there as here--surely we can *look on* in silence."

And on that agreement we all went to bed.

But on the following day, as we sat in the garden after dinner, our attempts to "keep off the grass" were miserably visible. They cast a constraint on the party. Every topic seemed to lead to the forbidden enclosure. It was at a very critical moment that the Sculptor, sitting cross-legged on a bench, in a real Alma Tadema attitude, filled the dangerous pause with:

"It was in the days of our Lord 1348 that there happened in Florence, the finest city in Italy--"

And the Violinist, who was leaning against a tree, touched an imaginary mandolin, concluding: "A most terrible plague."

The Critic leaped to his feet.

"A corking idea," he cried.

"Mine, mine own," replied the Sculptor. "I propose that what those who, in the days of the terrible plague, took refuge at the Villa Palmieri, did to pass away the time, we, who are watching the war approach--as our host says it will--do here. Let us, instead of disputing, each tell a story after dinner--to calm our nerves,--or otherwise."

At first every one hooted.

"I could never tell a story," objected the Divorcee.

"Of course you can," declared the Journalist. "Everybody in the world has one story to tell."

"Sure," exclaimed the Lawyer. "No embargo on subjects?"

"I don't know," smiled the Doctor. "There is always the Youngster."

"You go to blazes," was the Youngster's response, and he added: "No war stories. Draw that line."

"Then," laughed the Doctor, "let's make it tales of our own, our native land." And there the matter rested. Only, when we separated that night, each of us carried a sealed envelope containing a numbered slip, which decided the question of precedence, and it was agreed that no one but the story-teller should know who was to be the evening's entertainer, until story-telling hour arrived with the coffee and cigarettes.

I

THE YOUNGSTER'S STORY
IT HAPPENED AT MIDNIGHT
THE TALE OF A BRIDE'S NEW HOME

The daytimes were not ever very bad. Short-handed in the pretty garden, every one did a little work. The Lawyer was passionately fond of flowers, and the Youngster did most of the errands. The Sculptor had found some clay, and loved to surprise us at night with a new centre piece for the table, and the Divorcee spent most of her time tending Angele's baby, while the Doctor and the Nurse were eternally fussing over new kinds of bandages and if ever we got together, it was usually for a little reading aloud at tea-time, or a little music. The spirit of discussion seemed to keep as far away before the lights were up as did the spirit of war, and nothing could be farther than that *appeared*.

The next day we were unusually quiet.

Most of us kept in our rooms in the afternoon. There were those stories to think over, and that we all took it so seriously proved how very much we had been needing some real thing to do. We got through dinner very comfortably.

There was little news in the papers that day except enthusiastic accounts of the reception of the British troops by the French. It was lovely to see the two races that had met on so many battle fields--conquered, and been conquered by one another--embracing with enthusiasm. It was to the credit of all of us that we did not make the inevitable reflections, but only saw the humor and charm of the thing, and remembered the fears that had prevented the plans of tunnelling the channel, only to find them humorous.

The coffee had been placed on the table. The Trained Nurse, as usual, sat behind the tray, and we each went and took our cup, found a comfortable seat in the circle under the trees, where a few yellow lanterns swung in the soft air.

Then the Youngster pulled a white head-band with a huge "Number One" on it, out of his pocket, placed it on his head after the manner of the French Conscripts, struck an attitude in the middle of the circle, drew his chair deftly under him, and with the air of an experienced monologist began:

*   *   *   *   *

Not so very many years ago there was a pretty wedding at Trinity Church in Boston. It was quite the sort of marriage Bostonians believe in. The man was a rising lawyer, rather a sceptic on all sorts of questions, as most of us chaps pride ourselves on being, when we come out of college. They were married in church to please the Woman. What odds did it make?

Before they were married they had decided to live outside the city. She wanted a garden and an old house. He did not care where they lived so long as they lived together. Very proper of him, too. They spent the last year of their engaged life, the nicest year of some girls' lives, I have heard--in hunting the place. What they finally settled on was an old colonial house with a colonnaded front, and a round tower at each end, standing back from the road, and approached by a wide circular drive. It was large, substantial, with great possibilities, and plenty of ground. It had been unoccupied for many years, and the place had an evil report, and, at the time when they first saw it, appeared to deserve it.

He had looked it over. The situation was healthy. It was convenient to the city. He could make it in his car in less than forty-five minutes. They saw what could be done with the place, and did not concern themselves with *why* other people had not cared to live there. Architects, interior decorators, and landscape gardeners were put to work on it, and, even before the wedding, the place was well on toward its habitable stage.

Then they were married, and, quite correctly, went abroad to float in a gondola on the Grand Canal--together; to cross the Gemmi--together; to stroll about Pompeii and cross to Capri--together; and then ravage antiquity shops in Paris-- together. They returned in the early days of a glorious September. The house was ready for its master and mistress to lay the touch of their personality on it, and put in place the trophies of their Wedding Journey.

The evil look the house once had was gone.

A few old trees had been cut down round it to let in the glorious autumn sun all over the house, and when, on their first morning, after a good sound, well-earned sleep, they took their coffee on the terrace off the breakfast room, under a yellow awning, they certainly did not think, if they ever had, of the mysterious rumors against the house which had been whispered about when they first bought it. To them it seemed that they had never seen a gayer place.

But on the second night, just as the Woman was putting her book aside, and had a hand stretched out to shut off the light, she stopped--a carriage was com- ing up the drive. She sat up, and listened for the bell. It did not ring. After a few moments--as there was absolutely no sound of the carriage passing--she got up, and gently pushed the shutter--her room was on the front--there was nothing there, so, attaching no importance to it, she went quietly to bed, put out her light, just noticing as she did so, that it was midnight, and went to sleep. In the morning, the incident made so little impression on her, that she forgot to even mention it.

The next night, by some queer trick of memory, just as she went to bed, the thing came back to her, and she was surprised to find that she had no sleep in her. Instead of that she kept looking at the clock, and just before twelve, cold chills began to go down her back, when she heard the rapid approach of a carriage--this time she was conscious that her hearing was so keen that she knew there were two horses. She listened intently--no doubt about it--the carriage had stopped at the door.

Then there was a silence.

She was just convincing herself that there must be some sort of echo which made it appear that a team passing in the road had come up the drive--when she was suddenly sure that she heard a hurried step in the corridor--it passed the door. Now she was naturally a very unimaginative person, and had never had occasion to know fear. So, after a bit, she put out her light, saying to herself that a belated servant was busy with some neglected work--nothing more likely--and she went to sleep.

Again the morning sunlight, the Man's gay companionship, the hundreds of delightful things to do, wiped out that bad quarter of an hour, and again it never occurred to her to mention it.

The next night the remembrance came back so vividly after the Man had gone to his room, that she regretted she had not at least asked him if he had heard a carriage pass in the night. Of course she was sure that he had not. He was such a sound sleeper. Besides, it was not important. If he had, he would not have been nervous about it. Still, she could not sleep, and, just before the dining room clock began to chime midnight--she had never heard it before, and that she heard it now was a proof of how her whole body was listening--again came the rapid tread of running horses. This time every hair stood up on her head, and before she could control herself, she called out toward the open door: "Dearest, are you awake?"

Almost before she had the words out he was standing smiling in the doorway. It was all right.

"Did you *think* you heard a carriage come up the driveway?" she asked.

"Why, yes," he replied, "but I didn't."

"Listen! Is there some one coming along the corridor?"

He crossed the room quietly, opened the door, and turned on the light. "No, dear. There is no one there."

"Hadn't you better ring for your man, and have him see if any of the servants are up?"

He sat down on the edge of the bed, and laughed heartily.

"See here, dear girl," he said, "you and I are a pair of healthy people. We have happened to hear a noise which we can't explain. Be sure that there is rational explanation. You're not afraid?"

"Well, no, I really am not," she declared, "but you cannot deny that it is strange. Did you hear it last night?"

"Go on, now, with your cross-examination," he said. "Let's go to sleep. At any rate the exhibition is over for to-night."

The fourth night they did not speak in the night any more than they had in the daytime. But the next day they had a long conversation, the gist of which was this: That they had bought the place, that except for fifteen minutes at midnight, the place was ideal. They were both level-headed, neither believed in anything super-natural. Were they to be driven out of such a place by so harmless a thing as an unexplained noise? They could get used to it. After a bit it would no more wake them up,--such was the force of habit--than the ticking of the clock. To all this they both agreed, and the matter was dropped.

For ten days they did not mention it, but in all those ten days a sort of crescendo of emotion was going on in her. At first she began to think of it as soon as bed-time approached; then she felt it intruding on her thoughts at the dinner table; then she was unable to sleep for an hour or two after the fifteen minutes had passed, and, finally, one night, she fled into his room to find him wide awake, just before dawn, and to confess that the shadow of midnight was stretched before and after until it was almost a black circle round the twenty-four hours.

She knew it was absurd. She had no intention of being driven out of such a lovely place--BUT--

"See here, dear," he said. "Let's break our rule. We neither of us want company, but let's, at least, have a big week ender, and perhaps we can prove to ourselves that our nerves are wrong. One thing is sure, if you are going to get pale over it, I'll burn the blooming house down before we'll live in it."

"But you mind it yourself?"

"Not a bit!"

"But you are awake."

"Of course I am, because I know that you are."

"Do you mean to say that if I slept you wouldn't notice it?"

"On my honor--I should not."

"You are a comfort," she ejaculated. "I shall go right to sleep." And off she went, and did go to sleep.

All the same, in the morning, he insisted on the house-party.

"Let me see our list," he said. "Let us have no students of occult; no men who dabble in laboratory spiritualism; just nice, live, healthy people who never heard of such things--if possible. You can find them."

"You see, dear," she explained, "it would not trouble me if I heard it and you did not--but--"

"Oh, fudge!" he laughed. "Just now I should be sure to hear anything you did, I suppose."

"You old darling," she replied, "then I don't care for it a bit."

"All the same we'll have the house-party."

So the following Saturday every room in the house was occupied.

At midnight they were all gathered in the long drawing room opening on the colonnade, and, when the hour sounded, some one was singing. The host and hostess heard the running horses, as usual, and they were conscious that one or two people turned a listening ear, but evidently no one saw anything strange in it, and no comment was made. It was after one when they all went up to their rooms, so that evening passed off all right.

But on Sunday night two of the younger guests had gone to sit on the front terrace, and the older people were walking, in the moonlight, in the garden at the back. The sweet little girl, who was having her hand held, got up properly when she heard the carriage coming, and went to the edge of the terrace to see who was arriving at midnight. She had a fit of nerves as the invisible vehicle and its running horses seemed about to ride over her. She ran in, trembling with fear, to tell the tale, and of course every one laughed at her, and the matter would have been dropped, if it had not happened that, just at that moment a very pale gentleman came stumbling out of the house with the statement that he wanted a conveyance "to take him back to town," that "he refused to sleep in a haunted house," that he "had encountered an invisible person running along the corridor to his room," in fact the footsteps had as he put it "passed right through him."

The host broke into laughter, but he took the bull by the horns--the facts, as he knew them, were safer than the tales which he knew would run over the city if he attempted to deny things.

"See here, my good people," he said, "there is a little mystery here that we can't explain. The truth is, there *is* a story about this house. It used to belong to the president of a well-known railroad. That was twenty-five years ago. They say that one night, when he was driving from a place he had up country, his team was run into at a railway crossing five miles from here--one of those grade crossings that never ought to have been--and he was killed and his horses came home at midnight. 'They say' that the people who lived here after that declared that the horses have come home every midnight since. Now, there's the story. They don't do any harm. It only takes them a few minutes. They don't even trample the driveway, so why not?"

"All the same, I want to go back to town," said the frightened guest.

"I would stay the night, if I were you," said the host. "They won't come again until to-morrow."

All the same, when morning came, every one skipped, and as the last of them drove away, the Woman put her hand through the Man's arm, and smiled as she said: "It's all over. I don't mind a bit. When I heard you saying last night, 'They don't even trample the driveway, so why not?' I said to myself, 'Why not?' indeed."

"Good girl," he replied. "I'll bet my top hat you grow to be proud of them."

I don't know that they ever did, but I do know that they still live there. I went to school with the son, and whenever any one bragged, he used to say, "Well, we've *always* had a ghost. You ain't got that!"

The Youngster threw his lighted cigarette into the air, ran under it, caught it between his lips, and made a bow, as the Doctor broke into a roar of laughter.

"I know that old house," he said. "Jamaica Pond. But see here, Youngster, your idea of ghosts is terribly illogical. It was the *man* who was killed, not the *horses*. The wrong part of the team walked."

"You *are* particular," replied the Youngster. "The man did not come back, and the horses did. I can't split hairs when it's a ghost story. I feel afraid that I have missed my vocation, and that flights in the imagination are more in my line than flights in the air. I don't know what you think. *I* think it's a mighty good story. I say, Journalist, do you think I could sell that story? I've never earned a dollar in my life."

"Well," laughed the Journalist, "a dollar is just about what you would get for it."

"If I had been doing that story," said the Critic, "I should have found a logical explanation for it."

"Of course you would," said the Youngster. "I know one of a haunted house on St. James Street which had an explanation."

But the Doctor cut him short with: "Come now, you've done your stunt. No more stories to-night. Off to bed. You and I are going to take a run to Paris to-morrow."

"What for?"

"Tell you to-morrow."

As every one began to move toward the house, the Violinist remarked, "I was thinking of running up to Paris myself to-morrow. Any one else want to go with me?" The Journalist said that he did, and the party broke up. As they strolled toward the house the Lawyer was heard asking the Youngster, "What were the steps in the corridor?"

"Well," replied the Youngster, "I suppose on the night that the team came home there must have been great excitement in the house--every one running to and fro and--"

But the Journalist's shout of laughter stopped him.

The Youngster eyed him with shocked surprise.

"By Jupiter!" cried the Journalist. "That is the darnedest ghost story I ever heard. Everything and everybody walked but the dead man--even the carriage."

"That isn't *my* fault," said the Youngster, indignantly.

II

THE TRAINED NURSE'S STORY
THE SON OF JOSEPHINE
THE TALE OF A FOUNDLING

The house was very quiet next day. All the men, except the Critic and the Sculptor, had made an early and hurried run to Paris. So we saw little of each other until we gathered for dinner, and the conversation was calm-- in fact subdued.

The Doctor was especially quiet. No one was really gay except the Youngster. He talked of what he had seen in Paris--the silent streets--the moods of the women--the sight of officers in khaki flying about in big touring cars--and no one asked what had really taken them to town.

The Trained Nurse and I had walked to the nearest village, but we brought back little in the way of news. The only interesting thing we saw was *Monsieur le Cure* talking to a handsome young peasant woman in the square before the church. We heard her say, with a sob in her throat, "If my man does not come back, I'll never say my prayers again. I'll never pray to a God who let this thing happen unless my man comes back."

"She will, just the same," said the Lawyer. "One of the strangest features of such a catastrophe is that it steadies a race, especially the race convinced that it has right on its side."

"It goes deeper than that," said the Journalist. "It strikes millions with the same pain, and they bear together what they could not have faced separately."

"True," remarked the Doctor, "and that is one reason why I have always mistrusted the effort of people outside the radius of disaster to help in anyway, except scientifically."

"That is rather a cruel idea," commented the Trained Nurse.

"Perhaps. But I believe organized charity even of that sort is usually ineffective, and weakens the race that accepts it. I believe victims of such disaster are healthier and come out stronger for facing it, dying, or surviving, as Fate decrees."

"Keep off the grass," cried the Youngster. "I brought back a car full of books." The hint was taken, and we talked of books until the coffee came out.

As usual, the Trained Nurse sat behind the pot, and when we were all served, she pushed the tray back, folded her strong capable white hands on the edge of the table, and said quietly:

"Messieurs et Mesdames"--

We lit our cigarettes, and she began:

*   *   *   *   *

It was the first year after I left home and took up nursing. I had a room at that time in one of the Friendly Society refuges on the lower side of Beacon Hill. It was under the auspices of an Episcopal High Church in the days of Father Hall, and was rather English in tone. Indeed its matron was an Englishwoman--gentle, round-faced, lace-capped, and very sympathetic. I was very fond of her. I had, as a seamstress, a neat little girl named Josephine.

Josephine was a tiny creature, all grey in tone, with mouse-colored hair. She was a foundling. She had not the least notion who her people were. Her first recollections were of the orphan asylum where she was brought up. In her early teens she had been bound out to a dressmaker, who had been kind to her, and, when her first employer died, Josephine, who had saved a little money, and longed for independence, began to go out as a seamstress among the women she had grown to know in the dressmaking establishment, and went to live at one of the Christian Association homes for working girls.

Every one knows what those boarding houses are--two or three hundred girls of all ages, from sixteen up, of all temperaments. All girls willing to submit to control; girls with their gay days and their tragic, girls of ambition, and girls with faith in the future, as well as girls of no luck, and girls with their simple youthful romances.

Every one loved Josephine.

She was by nature a little lady, dainty in her ways, industrious, unrebellious, always ready to help the other girls about their clothes, and a model of a confidant. Every one told her their little troubles, every one confided their little romances. They were sure of a good listener, who never had any troubles or romances of her own to confide.

I don't know how old Josephine was at that time. She might have been twenty-five, looked younger, but was perhaps older. She was so tiny, and such a mouse of a thing that she seemed a child, but for her energy, and her capacity for silence.

It was, I fancy, three years after I first knew her that she one evening confided to a group of her intimate friends, as they sat together over their sewing, that she was engaged to be married. There was a great excitement. Little lonely Josephine, so discreet, who had sympathized with the romances of so many of her comrades, had a romance of her own. Such a hugging and kissing as went on, you never saw, unless you have seen a crowd of such girls together. Every one was full of questions, and there were almost as many tears shed as questions asked.

He was a carpenter, Josephine told them. She had known him ever since she was with the dressmaker who took her out of the asylum. He lived in Utica, New York. He had a good job, and they were to be married as soon as she could get ready.

So Josephine set to work with her nimble fingers to make her trousseau. During the years she had worked for me, the Matron at the Friendly Society, and many of its patrons had come to know and love dear little Josephine, and in our house there was almost as much excitement over the news as there was at the Association at the South End. All the girls set to work to make something for little Josephine. Every one for whom she had worked gave her something. One lady gave her black silk for a frock. All the girls sewed a bit of underwear for her. She had sheets and table linen, and all sorts of dainty things which her girl friends loved to count over, and admire in the evening without the least bit of envy. By the time Spring came

Josephine had to buy a new trunk to pack her things away in.

Then she told us all that she was going to Utica to be married. What was the use of his spending his money to come east for her, and pay his expenses back? That seemed reasonable, and the day was fixed for her departure.

Her trunks were packed.

She took a night train so that we could all go to the station to see her off, and I am sure that the crowd who saw us kissing her good-bye are not likely to forget the scene.

Then the girls went home chattering about "dear little Josephine."

In due time came a letter from a place near Utica, where she was, she said, on her little "wedding trip," and "very happy," and "he" sent his love, and it was signed with her new name, and she would send us her address as soon as she was settled.

Time went by--some months. Then she did send an address, but she did not write often, and when she did, she said little but that she was happy.

As nearly as I can remember, it was a year and a half after she left that news came that Josephine had a son. By that time a great many of the girls she had known were gone. Changes come fast in such a place. But there was great rejoicing, and those who had known her found time to make something for dear little Josephine's baby, and the sending of the things kept up the interest in her for some months.

Then the letters ceased again.

I can't be sure how long it was after that that I received a letter from her. She told me that her husband was dead, that she never really had taken root in Utica, and now that she was alone, with her baby to support, she longed to come back to Boston, and asked my advice. Did I think she could take up her old work?

I took the letter at once to the Matron of the Friendly Society--I happened to be resting between two cases--and we decided that it was safe. At least between us we could help her make the trial.

A few months later she came, and we went to the station to meet her. I could not see that she had changed a bit. She did not look a day older, and the bouncing baby she carried in her arms was a darling.

Of course she could not go back to the Association. That was not for married women. But we found her a room just across the street, and in no time, she dropped right back into the place she had left. Every morning she took the baby boy to the *creche* and every night she took him home, and a better cared-for, better loved, more wisely bred youngster was never born, nor a happier one. Every one loved him just as every one loved Josephine.

There I thought Josephine's story ended, and so far as she was concerned, it did.

But when the baby was six years old, and forward for his age, the Matron of the Friendly Society came into my room one day, when I was there to take a longer rest than usual, after a very trying case, and told me that she was in great distress. A friend of hers, who had been her predecessor, and was now the Matron of an Orphan Asylum in New York State, was going to the hospital to have a cataract removed from her eye, and had written to ask her to come and take her place while she was away. She begged me to replace her at the Friendly Society while she was gone. As her assistant was a capable young woman, and my relations with every one were pleasant I was only too glad to consent. She had always been so good to me.

She was gone a month.

On her return I noticed that she was distressed about something. I taxed her with it. She said it was nothing she felt like talking about. But one evening when Josephine had been sewing for me, after she was gone, the Matron, who had been in my room, got up, and closed the door after her.

"I've really got to tell you what is on my mind," she said. "And I am sure that you will look on it as a confidence. You know the asylum where I have been is not far from Utica, where Josephine went when she was married. Well, one day, about a fortnight after I got there, I had occasion to look up the record of a child in the books, and my attention was attracted by a name the same as Josephine's. The co-incidence struck me, and I read the record that on a certain day, which as near as I could calculate, must have been a year after Josephine left, a person of her name, written down as a widow, a member of the Orthodox Church, had adopted a male child a few months old. I was interested. I did not suspect anything, but I asked the assistant matron if she remembered the case. She did, clearly. She said the woman was a dear little thing, who had come there shortly before, a young widow, a seam-stress. She was a lonely little thing, and some one connected with the asylum had given her work, which she had done so well that she soon had all she needed. She had been employed in the asylum, and loved children as they did her. The child in question was the son of a woman who had died at its birth, from the shock of an accident which had killed the father. It took a fancy to Josephine, and she wanted to adopt it. The committee took the matter up. The clergyman spoke well of her, as did every one, and they all decided that she was perfectly able to care for it. So she took the child. All of a sudden, one day, Josephine went, as she had come. There was no mystery about it. She told the clergyman that she was homesick for her old friends, and had gone east, and would write, and she always has.

"Of course I was puzzled. There was no doubt in my mind that it was our little Josephine. Naturally I was discreet. Luckily. I spoke of her to several people who remembered her, and they all called her 'dear little Josephine' just as we had. I talked of her with the clergyman and his wife. I asked questions that were too natural to rouse suspicions, when I told them that I knew her, that the baby was the dearest and happiest child I knew, and what do you suppose I found out, more by inference than facts?"

No need to ask me. Didn't I know?

Josephine had never been married. There had never been any "He." It all seemed so natural. It did not shock me, as it had the Matron, and I was glad she had told no one but me. Dear little Josephine! Sitting there in the Association without family, with no friends but her patrons, and those girls whose little romances went on about her! No romances ever came her way. So she had made one all of her own. I proved to the Matron easily that what she had discovered by accident was not her affair, that to keep Josephine's secret was a virtue, and not a sin. I was sure of that, for, as I watched her afterwards, I knew that Josephine had played her part in her dream romance so well, that she no longer remembered that it was not true. She had forgotten she had not really borne the child she carried so lovingly in her arms.

*   *   *   *   *

"Is that all?" asked the Journalist.

"That is all," replied the Trained Nurse.

"By Jove," said the Doctor, "that is a good story. I wish I had told it."

"Thank you, Doctor," laughed the Trained Nurse. "I thought it was a bit in your line."

"But fancy the cleverness of the little thing to do all the details up so nicely," said the Lawyer. "She dovetailed everything so neatly. But what I want to know is whether she planned the baby when she planned the make-believe husband?"

"I fancy not," replied the Nurse. "One thing came along after another in her imagination, quite naturally."

"Poor little Josephine--it seems to me hard luck to have had to imagine such an every day fate," sighed the Divorcee.

"Don't pity her," snapped the Doctor. "Poor little Josephine, indeed! Lucky little Josephine, who arranged her own romance, and risked no disillusion. There have been cases where the joys of the imagination have been more dangerous."

"You are sure she had no disillusion?" asked the Critic.

"I am," said the Nurse.

"And her name was Josephine?" asked the Divorcee.

"It was not, and Utica was not the town," replied the Nurse.

"Perhaps her disillusion is ahead of her," said the Journalist. "'Say no man'--or woman either--'is happy until the day of his death.'"

"She *is* dead," said the Nurse.

"I told you she was lucky little Josephine," ejaculated the Doctor.

"And she died without telling the boy the truth?" asked the Journalist.

"The truth?" repeated the Nurse. "I've told you that she had forgotten it. No woman was ever so loved by a son. No mother ever so grieved for."

"Then the son lives?" asked the Doctor.

The Nurse smiled quietly.

"Good-night," said the Doctor. "I am going to bed to dream of that. It is a pity some of the rest of us childless slackers had not done as well as Josephine. She took her risk. She was lucky."

"She did," replied the Nurse, "but she did not realize anything of that. She was too simple, too unanalytic."

"I wonder?" said the Critic.

"You need not, I know." Her eyes fell on the Lawyer, and she caught a laugh in his eye. "What does that mean?" she asked.

"Well," said the Lawyer, "I was only thinking. She was religious, that dear little

Josephine?"

"At least she always went to church."

"I know the type," said the Violinist, gently. "Accepted what she was taught, believed it."

"Exactly," said the Lawyer, "that is what I was getting at. Well then, when her son meets her *au dela*--he will ask for his father--"

"Or," interrupted the Violinist, "his own mother will claim him."

"Don't worry," laughed the Critic. "It's dollars to doughnuts that she was 'dear little Josephine' to all the Heavenly Host half an hour after she entered the 'gates of pearl.' Don't look shocked. That is not sacrilegious. It is intentions--motives, that are immortal, not facts. Besides--"

"Don't push that idea too far," interrupted the Doctor from the door.

"Don't be alarmed. I was only going to say--there are Ik Marvels *au dela*--"

"I knew that idea was in your head. Drop it!" laughed the Doctor.

"Anyway," said the Violinist, "if Life is but a dream, she had a pretty one. Good night." And he went up to bed, and we all soon followed him, and I imagine not one of us, as we looked out into the moonlit air, thought that night of war.

III

THE CRITIC'S STORY
'TWAS IN THE INDIAN SUMMER
THE TALE OF AN ACTRESS

The next day, just as we were sitting down to dinner, the news came that Namur had fallen. The German army had marched singing into the burning town the afternoon before. The Youngster had his head over a map almost all through dinner. The Belgians were practically pushed out of all but Antwerp, and the Germans were rapidly approaching the natural defences of France running from Lille to Verdun, through Valenciennes, Mauberge, Hirson and Mezieres.

Things were beginning to look serious, although we still insisted on believing that the Germans could not break through. One result of the march of events was that we none of us had any longer the smallest desire to argue. Theories were giving way to the facts of every day, but in our minds, I imagine, we were every one of us asking, "How long CAN we stay here? How long will it be wise, even if we are permitted?" But, as if by common consent, no one asked the question, and we were only too glad to sit out in the garden we had all learned to love, and to talk of anything which was not war, until the Critic moved his chair into the middle of the circle, and began his tale.

"Let me see," he remarked. "I need a property or two," and he pulled an envelope out of his pocket and laid it on the table, and, leaning his elbows on it, began:

*   *   *   *   *

It was in the Autumn of '81 that I last saw Dillon act.

She had made a great success that winter, yet, in the middle of the season, she had suddenly disappeared.

There were all kinds of newspaper explanations.

Then she was forgotten by the public that had enthusiastically applauded her, and which only sighed sadly, a year later, on hearing of her death, in a far off Italian town,--sighed, talked a little, and forgot again.

It chanced that a few years later I was in Italy, and being not many miles from the town where I heard that she was buried, and a trifle overstrung by a few months delicious, aimless life in that wonderful country, I was taken with a sentimental fancy to visit her grave.

It was a sort of pilgrimage for me, for I had given to Dillon my first boyish devotion.

I thought of her, and to remember her was to recall her rare charm, her beauty, her success, after a long struggle, and the unexpected, inexplicable manner in which she had abandoned it. It was to recall, too, the delightful evenings I had spent under her influence, the pleasure I had had in the passion of her "Juliet," the poetic charm of her "Viola"; the graceful witchery of her "Rosalind"; how I had smiled with her "Portia"; laughed with her "Beatrice"; wept with her "Camille"; in fact how I had yielded myself up to her magnetism with that ecstatic pleasure in which one gets the best joys of every passion, because one does not drain the dregs of any.

I well remembered her last night, how she had disappeared, how she had gone to Europe, how she had died abroad,--all mere facts known in their bareness only to the public.

It was hard to find the place where she was buried. But at last I succeeded.

It was in a humble churchyard. The grave was noticeable because it was well kept, and utterly devoid of the tawdry ornamentation inseparable from such places in Italy. It was marked by a monument distinctly unique in a European country. It was a huge unpolished boulder, over which creeping green vines were growing.

On its rough surface a cross was cut, and underneath were the words:

"Yesterday This Day's Madness did prepare,
To-morrow's Silence, Triumph or Despair."

Below that I read with stupefaction,

"Margaret Dillon and child,"

and the dates
"January, 1843" "July 25, 1882."

In spite of the doubts and fancies this put into my mind, I no sooner stood beside the spot where the earth had claimed her, than all my old interest in her returned. I lingered about the place, full of romantic fancies, decorating her tomb with flowers, as I had once decorated her triumphs, absorbed in a dreamy adoration of her memory, and singing her praise in verse.

It was then that I learned the true story of her disappearance, guessed at that of her death, as I did at the identity of the young Dominican priest, who sometimes came to her grave, and who finally told me such of the facts as I know. I can best tell the story by picturing two nights in the life of Margaret Dillon, the two following her last appearance on the stage.

The play had been "Much Ado."

Never had she acted with finer humor, or greater gaiety. Yet all the evening she had felt a strange sadness.

When it was all over, and friends had trooped round to the stage to praise her, and trooped away, laughing and happy, she felt a strange, sad, unused reluctance to see them go.

Then she sat down to her dressing table, hurriedly removed her make-up, and allowed herself to be stripped of her stage finery. Her fine spirits seemed to strip off with her character. She shivered occasionally with nervousness, or superstition, and she was strangely silent.

All day she had, for some inexplicable reason, been thinking of her girlhood, of what her life might have been if, at a critical moment, she had chosen a woman's

ordinary lot instead of work,--or if, at a later day, she had yielded to, instead of re-
sisted, a great temptation. All day, as on many days lately, she had wondered if she
regretted it, or if, the days of her great triumph having passed,--as pass they must,-
-she should regret it later if she did not yet.

It was probably because,--early in the season as it was--she was tired, and the
October night oppressed her with the heat of Indian Summer.

Silently she had allowed herself to be undressed, and redressed in great haste.
But before she left the theatre she bade every one "good night" with more than her
usual kindliness, not because she did not expect to see them all on Monday,--it was
a Saturday night,--but because, in her inexplicably sad humour, she felt an irresistible desire to be at peace with the world, and a still deeper desire to feel herself
beloved by those about her.

Then she entered her carriage and drove hurriedly home to the tiny apartment
where she lived quite alone.

On the supper table lay a note.

She shivered as she took it up. It was a handwriting she had been accustomed to
see once a year only, in one simple word of greeting, always the same word, which
every year in eighteen had come to her on New Year's wherever she was.

But this was October.

She sat perfectly still for some minutes, and then resolutely opened the letter,
and read:

"Madge:--I am so afraid that my voice coming to you, not   only across so
many years, but from another world, may shock   you, that I am strongly tempted
not to keep my word to you,   yet, judging you by myself, I feel that perhaps this
will be   less painful than the thought that I had passed forgetful of   you, or
changed toward you. You were a mere girl when we   mutually promised, that
though it was Fate that our paths   should not be the same, and honorable that we
should keep   apart, we would not pass out of life, whatever came, without   a
farewell word,--a second saying 'good-bye.'"

"Madge:--I am so afraid that my voice coming to you, not
only across so many years, but from another world, may shock
you, that I am strongly tempted not to keep my word to you,

yet, judging you by myself, I feel that perhaps this will be less painful than the thought that I had passed forgetful of you, or changed toward you. You were a mere girl when we mutually promised, that though it was Fate that our paths should not be the same, and honorable that we should keep apart, we would not pass out of life, whatever came, without a farewell word,--a second saying 'good-bye.'"

"It is my fate to say it. It is now God's will. Before it was yours. It is eighteen years since you chose my honor to your happiness and mine. To-day you are a famous woman. That is the consolation I have found in your decision. I sometimes wonder if Fame will always make up to you for the rest. A woman's way is peculiar--and right, I suppose. I have never changed. My son has been a second consolation, and that, too, in spite of the fact that, had he never been born, your decision might have been so different. He is a young man now, strangely like what I was, when as a child, you first knew me, and he has always been my confidant. In those first days of my banishment from you I kept from crying my agony from the housetops by whispering it to him. His uncomprehending ears were my sole confessional. His mother cared little for his companionship, and her invalidism threw him continually into my care. I do not know when he began to understand, but from the hour he could speak he whispered your name in his prayers. But it was only lately that, of himself, he discovered your identity. The love I felt for you in my early days has grown with me. It has survived in my heart when all other passions, all prides, all ambitions, long ago died. I leave you, I hope, a good memory of me--a man who loved you more than he loved himself, who for eighteen years has loved you silently, yet never ceased to grieve for you. But I fear that I have

bequeathed to my son, with the name and estate of his
father, my hopeless love for you. If, by chance, what I fear
be true,--if, when bereft of me, he seeks you out, as be
sure he will,--deal gently with him for his father's sake.

"There was an old compact between us, dear. I mention it now
only in the hope that you may not have forgotten--indeed,
in the certainty that you have not. I know you so well.
Remember it, I beg of you, only to ignore it. It was made,
you know, when one of us expected to watch the passing of
the other. This is different. If this reminds you of it, it
reminds you only to warn you that Time cancels all such
compacts. It is my voice that assures you of it.

"FELIX R."

Underneath, written in letters, like, yet so unlike, were the words, "My father
died this morning. F. R." and an uncertain mark as though he had begun to add "Jr."
to the signature, and realized that there was no need.

The letter fell from her hands.

For a long time she sat silent.

Dead! She had never felt that he could die while she lived. A knowledge that he
was living,--loving her, adoring her hopelessly--was necessary to her life. She felt
that she could not go on without it. For eighteen years she had compared all other
men, all other emotions to him and his love, to find them all wanting.

And he had died.

She looked at the date of the letter. He would be resting in that tomb she remembered so well, before she could reach the place; that spot before which they
had often talked of Death, which had no terrors for either of them.

She rose. She pushed away her untouched supper, hurriedly drank a glass of
wine, and, crossing the hall to her bedroom, opened a tiny box that stood locked
upon her dressing table. She took from it a picture--a miniature. It was of a young
man not over twenty-five. The face was strong and full of virile suggestion, even in

a picture. The eyes were brown, the lips under the short mustache were firm, and the thick, short, brown hair fell forward a bit over the left temple. It was a handsome manly face.

The picture was dated eighteen years before. It hardly seemed possible that eighteen years earlier this woman could have been old enough to stir the passionate love of such a man. Her face was still young, her form still slender; her abundant hair shaded deep gray eyes where the spirit of youth still shone. But she belonged, by temperament and profession, to that race of women who guard their youth marvellously.

There were no tears in her eyes as she sat long into the morning, and, with his pictured face before her, reflected until she had decided.

He had kept his word to her. His "good bye" had been loyally said. She would keep hers in turn, and guard his first night's solitude in the tomb with her watchful prayers. She calculated well the time. If she travelled all day Sunday, she would be there sometime before midnight. If she travelled back at once, she could be in town again in season to play Monday; not in the best of conditions, to be sure, for so hard a role as "Juliet," but she would have fulfilled a duty that would never come to her again.

*   *   *   *   *

It was near midnight, on Sunday.

The light of the big round harvest moon fell through the warm air, which scarcely moved above the graves of the almost forgotten dead in the country churchyard. The low headstones cast long shadows over the long grass that merely trembled as the noiseless wind moved over it.

A tall woman in a riding dress stood beside the rough sexton at the door of the only large tomb in the enclosure.

He had grown into a bent old man since she last saw him, but he had recognized her, and had not hesitated to obey her.

As he unlocked and pushed back the great door which moved easily and noiselessly, he placed his lantern on the steps, and telling her that, according to a family custom, there were lights inside, he turned away, and left her, to keep his watch near by.

No need to tell her the family customs. She knew them but too well.

For a few moments she remained seated on the step where she had rested to await the opening of the door, on the threshold of the tomb of the one man among all the men she had met who had stirred in her heart a great love. How she had loved him! How she had feared that her love would wear his out! How she had suffered when she decided that love was something more than self-gratification, that even though for her he should put aside the woman he had heedlessly married years before, there could never be any happiness in such a union for either of them. How many times in her own heart she had owned that the woman would not have had the courage shown by the girl, for the girl did not realize all she was putting aside. Yet the consciousness of his love, in which she never ceased to believe, had kept her brave and young.

She rose and slowly entered the vault.

The odor of flowers, the odor of death was about it.

She lifted the lantern from the ground, and, with it raised above her head, approached the open coffin that rested on the catafalque in the centre of the tomb and mounted the two steps. She was conscious of no fear, of no dread at the idea of once more, after eighteen years, looking into the face of the man she had loved, who had carried a great love for her into another world. But as she looked, her eyes widened with fright. She bent lower over him. No cry burst from her lips, but the hand holding the lantern lowered slowly, and she tumbled down the two steps, and staggered back against the wall, where, behind lettered slides, the dead Richmonds for six generations slept their long sleep together. Her breast heaved up and down, as if life, like a caged thing, were striving to escape. Yet no sound came from her colorless lips, no tears were in her widened eyes.

The realizing sense of departed years had reached her heart at last, and the shock was terrible. With a violent effort she recovered herself. But the firm step, the fearless, hopeful face with which she had approached the coffin of her dead lover were very different from the blind manner in which she stumbled back to his bier, and the hand which a second time raised the lantern trembled so that its wavering light shed an added weirdness on the still face, so strange to her eyes, and stranger still to her heart.

He had been a young man when they parted. To her he had remained young. Now the hair about the brows was thin and white, the drooping mustache that entirely concealed the mouth was grizzled; lines furrowed the forehead, outlined the sunken eyes, and gave an added thinness to the nostrils. She bent once more over the face, to her only a strange cold mask. A painful fascination held her for several minutes, forcing her to mark how love, that had kept her young, proud, content in its very existence, had sapped his life, and doubled his years.

The realization bent her slender figure under a load of self-reproach and self-mistrust. She drooped lower and lower above the sad, dead face until she slid to the ground beside him. Heavy tearless sobs shook her slight frame as it stretched its length beside the dead love and the dead dream. The ideal so long treasured in her soul had lost its reality. The present had wiped out the past as a sponge wipes off a slate.

If she had but heeded his warning, and refrained from coming until later, she would have escaped making a stranger of him forever. Now the sad, aged face, the dead, strange face which she had seen but five minutes before, had completely obscured in her memory the long-loved, young face that had been with her all these years. The spirit whose consoling presence she had thought to feel upholding her at this moment made no sign. She was alone in the world, bereft of her one supporting ideal, alone beside the dead body of one who was a stranger alike to her sight and her emotions; alone at night in an isolation as unexpected as it was terrible to her, and which chilled her senses as if it had come to oppress her forever.

The shadows which she had not noticed before, the dark corners of the tomb, the motionless gleam of the moon as it fell through the open door, and laid silently on the floor like light stretched dead, the low rustle of the wind as if Nature restlessly moved in her sleep, came suddenly upon her, and brought her--fear. She held her breath as she stilled her sobs to realize that she alone lived in this city of the Dead. The chill of fright crept along the surface of her body, which still vibrated with her storm of grief.

She seemed paralyzed. She dared not move.

Every sense rallied to her ears in dread.

Suddenly she heard her name breathed: "Margaret!"

It was whispered in a voice once so familiar to her ears, a voice that used to say, "Madge."

She raised herself on her elbow.

She dared not answer.

She hardly dared breathe.

She was afraid in every sense, and yet she hungered for another sound of that loved voice. Every hour of its banishment was regretted at that moment. There seemed no future without it.

Every nerve listened.

At first she heard nothing but the restless moving of the air, which merely emphazied her loneliness, then she caught the pulsation of slow regular breathing.

She started to her feet.

She snatched up the lantern and quickly mounted to the bier. She looked sharply down into the dead face.

Silent, with its white hair, and worn lines, it rested on its white pillows.

No sound came from the cold still lips.

Yet, while her eyes were riveted on them, once more the longed-for voice breathed her name. "Margaret!"

It came from behind her.

She turned quickly.

There in the moonlit doorway, with a sad, compassionate smile on his strong, young face--as if it were yesterday they had parted--stood the man she remembered so well.

Her bewildered eyes turned from the silent, unfamiliar face among the satin cushions, to the living face in the moonlight,--the young, brown eyes, the short, brown hair falling forward over the left temple, the erect, elastic figure, the strong loving hands stretching out to her.

She was so tired, so heart sick, so full of longing for the love she had lost.

"Felix," she sobbed, and, blindly groping to reach what she feared was a hallucination, she stumbled down the steps, and was caught up in the arms flung wide to catch her, and which folded about her as if forever. She sighed his name again, upon the passionate young lips which had inherited the great love she had put aside so long before.

*   *   *   *   *

As the last words died away, the Critic drew himself up and laughed.

He had told the story very dramatically, reading the letter from the envelope he had called a "property," and he had told it well.

The laugh broke the spell, and the Doctor echoed it heartily.

"All right, old man," said the Critic, "you owed me that laugh. You're welcome."

"I was only thinking," said the Doctor, his face still on a broad grin, "that we have always thought you ought to have been a novelist, and now we know at last just what kind of a novelist you would have been."

"Don't you believe it," said the Critic, "That was only improvisatore--that's no sample."

"Ho, ho! I'll bet you anything that the manuscript is up in your trunk, and that you have been committing it to memory ever since this idea was proposed," said the Doctor, still laughing.

"No, *that* I deny," replied the Critic, "but as I am no *poseur*, I will own that I wrote it years ago, and rewrote it so often that I never could forget it. I'll confess more than that, the story has been 'declined with thanks' by every decent magazine in the States and in England. Now perhaps some one will tell me why."

"I don't know the answer," said the Youngster, seriously, "unless it is 'why not?'"

"I shouldn't wonder if it were sentimental twaddle," sighed the Journalist, "but I don't *know*."

"I noticed," expostulated the Critic, "that you all listened, enthralled."

"Oh," replied the Doctor, "that was a tribute to your personal charm. You did it very well."

"Exactly," said the Critic, "if editors would let me read them my stories, I could sell them like hot cakes. I never believed that Homer would have lived as long as he has, if he had not made the reputation of his tales by singing them centuries before any one tried to read them. Now no one *dares* to say they bore him. The reading public, and the editors who cater to it, are just like some stupid theatrical managers I know of, who will never let an author read a play to them for fear that he may give the play some charm that the fool theatrical man might not have felt from mere type-written words on white or yellow paper. By Jove, I know the case of a manager who once bought the option on a foreign play from a scenario provided by a clever friend of mine--and paid a stiff price for it, too, and when he got the manuscript wrote to the chap who did the scenario--'Play dashety-dashed rot. If it had been as good as your scenario, it would have gone.' And, what is more, he sacrificed the tidy five thousand he had paid, and let his option slide. Now, when the fellow who did the scenario wrote: 'If you found anything in the scenario that you did not discover in the play, it is because I gave you the effect it would have behind the footlights, which you have not the imagination to see in the printed words,' the Manager only replied 'You are a nice chap. I like you very much, but you are a blanketty-blanketty fool.'"

"Which was right?" asked the Journalist.

"The scenario man."

"How do you know?"

"How do I know? Why simply because the play was produced later--ran five years, and drew a couple of million dollars. That's how I know."

"By cricky," exclaimed the Youngster, "I believe he thinks his story could earn a million if it had a chance."

"I don't say 'no,'" said the Critic, yawning, "but it will never get a chance. I burned the manuscript this morning, and now being delivered of it, I have no more interest in it than a sparrow has in her last year's offspring."

"The trouble with you is that you haven't any patience, any staying power. That ought to have been a three volume novel. We would have heard all about their first meeting, their first love, their separation, his marriage, her *debuts*, etc., etc.," declared the Journalist.

"Oh, thunder," said the Doctor. "I think there was quite enough of it. Don't throw anything at me--I liked it--I liked it! Only I'm sorry she died."

"So am I," said the Critic. "That really hurt me."

"Because," said the Doctor, shying away toward the door, "I should have liked to know if the child turned out to be a genius. That kind do sometimes," and he disappeared into the doorway.

"Anyhow," said the Critic, "I am going to wear laurels until some one tells a better--and I'd like to know why the Journalist looks so pensively thoughtful?"

"I am trying to recall who she was--Margaret Dillon."

"Don't fret--she may be a 'poor thing,' but she is all 'mine own'--a genuine creation, Mr. Journalist. I am no reporter."

"Ah? Then you are more of a sentimentalist than I even dared to dream."

"Don't deny it," said the Critic, as he rose and yawned. "So I am going to bed to sleep on my laurels while I may. Good night."

"Well," called the Sculptor after him, as he sauntered away, "as one of our mutual friends used to say 'The Indian Summer of Passion scorches.'"

"But, alas!" added the other, "it does not **always** kill."

"Witness--" began the Journalist, but the Critic cut him short.

"As you love me--not that famous list of yours including so many of the actresses we all know. I can't bear THAT to-night. After all the French have a better phrase for it--'La Crise de quarante ans.'"

The Nurse and Divorcee had been very quiet, but here they locked hands, and the former remarked that they prepared to withdraw:

"That is our cue to disappear--and you, too, Youngster. These men are far too wise."

So we of the discussed sex made a circle with our clasped hand about the Youngster and danced him into the house. The last I saw of the garden that night, as I looked out of my window toward the northeast, with "Namur" beating in my head, the five men had their heads still together, but whether "the other sex" was getting scientifically torn to bits, or they, too, had Namur in their minds I never knew.

IV

THE DOCTOR'S STORY
AS ONE DREAMS
THE TALE OF AN ADOLESCENT

The next day was very peaceful. We were becoming habituated to the situation. It was a Sunday, and the weather was warm. There had been no real news so far as we knew, except that Japan had lined up with the Allies. The Youngster had come near to striking fire by wondering how the United States, with her dislike for Japan, would view the entering into line of the yellow man, but the spark flickered out, and I imagine we settled down for the story with more eagerness than on the previous evening, especially when the Doctor thrust his hands into his pockets and lifted his chin into the air, as if he were in the tribune. More than one of us smiled at his resemblance to Pierre Janet entering the tribune at the **College de France**, and the Youngster said, under his breath, "A **Clinique**, I suppose."

The Doctor's ears were sharp. "Not a bit," he answered, running his keen brown eyes over us to be sure we were listening before he began:

* * * * *

In the days when it was thought that the South End was to be the smart part of Boston, and when streets were laid out along wide tree shaded malls, with a square in the centre, in imitation of some quarters of London,--for Boston was in those days much more English in appearance than it is now,--there was in one of those squares a famous private school. In those days it was rather smart to go to a private school. It was in the days before Boston had much of an immigrant quarter, when some smart families still lived in the old Colonial houses at the North End, and ministers and lawyers and all professional men sent their sons and their daughters to the public schools, at that time probably the best in the world.

At this private school, there was, at the time of which I speak, what one might almost call a "principal girl."

She was the daughter of a rich banker--his only daughter. The gods all seemed to have been very good to her. She was not only a really beautiful girl, she was, for her age, a distinguished girl,--one of the sort who seemed to do everything better than any one else, and with a lack of self-consciousness or pretension. Every one admired her. Some of her comrades would have loved her if she had given them the chance. But no one could ever get intimate with her. She came and went from school quite alone, in the habit of the American girl of those days before the chaperon became the correct thing. She was charming to every one, but she kept every one a little at arm's length. Of course such a girl would be much talked over by the other type of girl to whom confidences were necessary.

As always happens in any school there was a popular teacher. She taught history and literature, and I imagine girls get more intimate with such a teacher than they ever do with the mathematics.

Also, as always happens, there was a "teacher's pet," one of those girls that has to adore something, and the literature teacher, as she was smart and good looking, was as convenient to adore as anything else,--and more adjacent.

Of course "teacher's pet" never has any secrets from the teacher, and does not mean to be a sneak either. Just can't help turning herself inside out for her idol, and when the heart of a girl of seventeen turns itself inside out, almost always something comes out that is not her business. That was how it happened that one day the literature teacher was told that the "Principal Girl" was receiving wonderful boxes of violets at the school door, and "Don't you know ONE DAY she was seen by a group of pupils who happened to be going home, and were just behind her, getting into a closed carriage and driving away from the corner of the street!"

Now the literature teacher did not, as a rule, encourage such confidences, but this time it seemed useful. She liked the Principal Girl--admired her, in fact. She was terribly shocked. She warned her pet to talk to no one else, and then she went at once to the clergyman who was at the head of the school. She knew that he felt responsible for his pupils, and this had an unpleasant look. He took the pains to verify the two statements. Then there was but one thing to do--to lay the matter before the parents of the girl.

Now, as so often happens in American families, the banker and his wife stood in some awe of their daughter. There was not that confidence between them which one traditionally supposes to exist between parents and children. I imagine that there is no doubt that the adolescent finds it much easier to confide in some one other than the parents who would seem to be her proper confidants.

At any rate the banker and his wife were simply staggered. They dared not broach the subject to the Principal Girl, and in their distress turned to the family lawyer. As they were too cowardly to take his first advice--perhaps they were afraid the daughter would lie, they sometimes do in the best regulated families,--it was decided to put a discreet person "on the job," and discover first of all what was really going on.

The result of the investigation was at first consoling, and then amazing.

They discovered that the bunches of violets were ordered at a smart down town florist by the girl herself, and by her order delivered at the school door by a liveried messenger boy, who, by her orders, awaited her arrival. As for the closed carriage, that she also bespoke herself at a smart livery stable where she was known. When she entered it, she was at once driven to the Park Street station, where she bought a round trip ticket to Waltham. There she walked to the river, hired a boat, rowed herself up stream, tied her boat at a wooden bank, climbed the slope, and sat there all the afternoon, sometimes reading, and sometimes merely staring out at the river, or up at the sky. At sunset she rowed back to the town, returned to the city, and walked from the station to her home.

This all seemed simple enough, but it puzzled the father, it made him unquiet in his mind. Why all this mystery? Why--well, why a great many things, for of course the Principal Girl had to prepare for these absences, and, although the little fibs she told were harmless enough--well, why? The literature teacher, who had been watching her carefully, had her theory. She knew a lot about girls. Wasn't she once one herself? So it was by her advice that the family doctor was taken into the family confidence, chiefly because neither father nor mother had the pluck to tackle the matter--they were ashamed to have their daughter know that she had been caught in even a small deception--it seemed so like intruding into her intimate life.

There are parents like that, you know.

The doctor had known the girl since he ushered her into the world. If there were any one with whom she had shown the slightest sign of intimacy, it was with him. Like all doctors whose associations are so largely with women, and who are moderately intelligent and temperamental, he knew a great deal about the dangers of the imagination. No one ever heard just what passed between the two. One thing is pretty sure, he made no secrets regarding the affair, and at the end of the interview he advised the parents to take the girl out of school, take her abroad, keep her active, present her at courts, show her the world, keep her occupied, interest her, keep her among people whether she liked it or not.

The literature teacher counted for something in the affair, and I imagine that it was never talked over between the parents and daughter, who soon after left town for Europe, and for three years were not seen in Boston.

When they *did* return, it was to announce the marriage of the Principal Girl to the son of the family lawyer, a clever man, and a rising politician.

Relations between the literature teacher and the Principal Girl had never wholly broken off, so ten years after the school adventure it happened one beautiful day in early September that the teacher was a guest at the North Shore summer home of the Principal Girl, now the mother of two handsome boys.

That afternoon at tea, sitting on the verandah, watching the white sails as the yachts made for Marblehead harbor, and the long line of surf beating against the rugged rocks beyond the wide pebbly beach on which the dragging stones made weird music, the literature teacher, supposing the old story to be so much ancient history that it could, as can so many of the incidents of one's teens, be referred to lightly, had the misfortune to mention it. To her horror, the Principal Girl gave her one startled look, and then rolled over among the cushions of the hammock in which she was swinging, and burst into a torrent of tears.

When the paroxysm had passed, she sat up, wiped her eyes in which, however, there was no laughter, and said passionately:

"I suppose you think me the most ungrateful woman in the world. I know only too well that to many women my position has always appeared enviable. Poor things, if they only knew! Of course, my husband is a good man. In all ways I do him perfect justice. He is everything that is kind and generous--only, alas, he is not the lover of my dreams. My children are nice handsome boys, but they are the every day children of every day life. I dreamed another and a different life in which my children were oh, so different, and beside which the life I try to lead with all the strength I have is no more like the life I dreamed than my boys are like my dream children. If you think it has not taken courage to play the part I have played, I am sorry for your lack of insight."

And she got up, and walked away.

It was as well, for, as the literature teacher told the doctor afterward, it was one notch above her experience, and she absolutely could have found no word to say. When the Wife came back to the hammock, ten minutes later, the cloud was gone from her face, and she never mentioned the subject again. And you may be sure that the literature teacher never did. She always looked upon the incident as her worst moment of tactlessness.

*   *   *   *   *

"Bully, bully!" exclaimed the Lawyer, "Take off your laurels, Critic, and crown the Doctor!"

"For that little tale," shouted the Critic. "Never! That has not a bit of literary merit. It has not one rounded period."

"The Lawyer is a realist," said the Sculptor. "Of course that appeals to him."

"If you want my opinion, I consider that there is just as much imagination in that story as in the morbid rigmarole you threw at us last night," persisted the Lawyer.

"Why," declared the Critic, "I call mine a healthy story compared with this one. It is a shocking tale for the operating room--I mean the insane asylum."

"All right," laughed the Doctor, "then we had all better go inside the sanitarium walls at once."

"Do you presume," said the Journalist, "to pretend that this is a normal incident?"

"I am not going into that. I only claim that more people know the condition than dare to confess it. It is after all only symbolic of the duality of the soul--or call it what you like. It is the embodiment of a truth which no one thinks of denying--that the spirit has its secrets. Imagination plays a great part in most of our lives--it is the glory that gilds our facts--it is the brilliant barrier which separates us from the beasts, and the only real thing that divides us into classes, though, of course, it does not run through the world like straight lines of latitude and longitude, but like the lines of mean temperature."

"The truth is," said the Lawyer, "if the Principal Girl had been obliged to struggle for her living, the fact that her imagination did not run at any point into her world of realities would not have been dangerous."

"Naturally not," said the Doctor, "for she would have been a great novelist, or a poor one, and all would have been well, or not, according to circumstances."

"All the same," persisted the Critic, "I think it a horrid story and--"

"I think," interrupted the Doctor, "that you have a vicious mind, and--" Here the Doctor cast a quick look in the direction of the Youngster, who was stretched out in a steamer chair and had not said a word.

"All right," said the Trained Nurse, "he is fast asleep." And so he was.

"Just as well," said the Doctor, "though it does not speak so well for the story as it might."

"Well," laughed the Journalist, "you have had a double success, Doctor. You have been spontaneously applauded by the man of law, and sent the man of the air to *faire dodo*. I reckon you get the laurels."

"Don't you be in such a hurry to award the palm," protested the Sculptor. "There are some of us who have not spoken yet. I am going to put some brilliant touches on mine before I give my star performance."

"What's that about stars?" yawned the Youngster, waking up slowly.

"Nothing except that you have given a very distinguished and unexpected star performance as a sleeper," said the Doctor.

"I say!" he exclaimed, sitting up. "By Jove, is the story of the Principal Girl all told? That's a shame. What became of her?"

"You'll never know now," said the Doctor.

"Besides," said the Critic, "you would not understand. You are too young."

"Well, I like your cheek."

"After all," said the Journalist, "it is only another phase of the Dear Little Josephine, and I still think that is the banner story."

"Me, too," said the Doctor, as we went into the house.

And I thought to myself, "I can tell a third phase--the tragic--when my turn comes," and I was the only one who knew that my story would come last.

V

THE SCULPTOR'S STORY
UNTO THIS END
THE TALE OF A VIRGIN

It was on August 26th that we were first sure that the Allied forces and the German army had actually come in contact. It seemed impossible for us to realize it, but, in the afternoon the Doctor, the Lawyer, and the Youngster took one of the cars, and made a run to the northeast. The news they brought back did not at all coincide with the hopeful tone of the morning papers. In fact it was not only evident that the fall of Namur had been followed almost immediately by that of Mons and Charleroi, but that the German hordes were well over the French frontier, and advancing rapidly, and the Allied armies simply flying before them.

The odd part was, that though the Youngster said that they had only run out fifty miles, they had heard the guns, and "the Doctor thinks," he added, under his breath, "that we may be able to stick it out to the last day of the month. Anyway, I advise you girls to look over your kits. We may fly in a hurry--such of us as must fly."

However, we managed to get through dinner quite gaily. We simply could not realize the menace, and the Doctor evidently meant that we should not. He was in gayer spirits than he had been since the days of the great discussions, and after the few facts he had brought back were given us, he kept the talk on other matters, until the Sculptor, who had been lying back in his chair, blowing smoke rings in the air, stretched himself into his most graceful position, and called attention even to his pose, before he threw his cigarette far from him with a fine gesture, settled his handsome head into his clasped hands, and began:

*   *   *   *   *

I had been ten years abroad.

In all that time I had been idle, prosperous, and wretched.

Every time Fate wrenched my heart with one of her long thin pitiless hands, she recompensed me with what the world calls "good luck." Every hope I had cherished failed me. Every faith I had harbored deserted me. Every venture in which neither heart nor soul was concerned flourished and flaunted its success in the face of the world, where I was considered a very fortunate man.

In the ten years of my exile I had travelled much, had been in contact with all kinds of people, had served some, and tried in vain to be concerned for them while I served. If it had been my fate to make no friends, it was within my choice to be never alone.

I had that in my memory which I hoarded, and yet with which I would not allow myself to be deliberately alone. The most terrible hours of my life were those when, toward morning, the rest of the world--all the world save me--having no past to escape, no enticing phantom to flee, went peacefully off to bed, and I was left alone in the night to drug memory, fight off thought, outwit imagination by any means that I might--and some of them were desperate enough.

Ten years had passed thus.

Another tenth of August had come round!

Only a man who has but one anniversary in his life, the backward and forward shadows of which make an unbroken circle over the whole year, can appreciate my existence. One cannot escape such a date. You may never speak of it. You may forswear calendars, abjure newspapers, refuse to date a letter; you may even lose days in a drunken stupor. Still there is that in your heart and your brain which keeps the reckoning. The hour will strike, in spite of you, when the day comes round on the dial of the year.

I had been living for some time in a city far distant from my native land. Half the world stretched on either side between me and the spot I tried to forget, and which floated forever, like a vision, between me and reality.

I had remained longer than usual in this city, for the simple reason that it was the hot season, and while the natives could stand it by day, visitors, unused to the heat, were forced to sleep by day and wander abroad by night, a condition that made it possible for me to feel my fellowmen about me nearly the entire twenty-four hours.

It was night.

I was sitting alone on the balcony of my room, looking down on to the crowded bridges of the city where throngs were passing, and filled my eyes and mind.

It was the very hour at which I had last seen her. There was no clock in sight--I always guarded against that in selecting my room. I had long ceased to carry a watch.

Yet I knew the hour.

I had been sitting there for hours watching the crowd. I had not been drinking. I had long ago abandoned that. No stimulant could blur the fixed regret, no narcotic numb my full sense of it. Sleep, whether I rose to it, or fell to it--only brought me dreams of her. Desperate nourishing of a great misery, in a nature that resented it, even while cherishing it, had made me a conscious monomaniac. Fate had thwarted me, and distorted me. I had become jealous and morbid, bitterly reviling my hurt, but violently preventing its healing.

There was a moon--just as there had been that night, only now it fell on a many bridged river across which were ghostly cypress trees, rising along the hillside to a strangely outlined church behind ruined fortifications. I was wondering, against my will, at what hour that moon rose over the distant New England village, which came before me in a vision that wiped out the wooded heights of reality.

Suddenly all the pain dropped away from me.

I drew a long breath in amazement.

Where was the weight under which I had staggered, mentally, all these years? Whence came the peace that had so suddenly descended upon me? In an instant it had passed, and I could only remember my bitter mood of ten years as if it had been a dream that I had lived so long unconsoled by that great healer, Time.

As the torturing jealousy dropped from me, a gentle sadness took its place. In an instant my mind was made up. I would go back.

This idea, which had never come to me in ten years, seemed now perfectly natural. I would return at once to that far off village where, for a brief hour, I had dwelt in a "Fool's Paradise," through which my way had lain but a brief span, and where I had passed, like the fabled bird, that "floats through Heaven, but cannot light."

*   *   *   *   *

I remember but little of the journey home, save that it was long, and that I slept much. But whether it was months or years I never knew. I seemed to be making up what I had lost in ten years. Time occupied itself in restoring the balance I had taken so much pains to upset.

It was night when I reached the place at last.

I found it as I had left it. Had a magic sleep settled there it could not have been less changed.

I was recognized in the small bare office of the one tavern. I felt that my sudden appearance surprised no one. But I did not wonder why.

Oddly enough, I never asked a question. I had not even questioned myself as to what I expected to find. Years afterward I was convinced, in reviewing the matter, that my soul had known from the first.

I dined alone, quite calmly, after which I stepped out into the starlight. I turned up the hill, and struck into the familiar road I had so often travelled in the old days. It led toward the river, and along the steep bank of the rapid noisy stream. The chill wind of an early autumn night moaned sadly in the tall trees, and the dead leaves under my feet rustled a sad accompaniment to my thoughts, which at last, unhooded, flew back to the past.

Below rushed the river, whose torrent had ever been an accompaniment to all my recollections of her--as inseparable from them as the color of her eyes, or the tones of her voice.

I could not but contrast my present calm with the mad humor in which I had last rushed down the slope I was so quietly climbing. As I went forward, I began to ask myself, "Why?" I could not answer that, but I began to hurry.

Suddenly I stopped.

The moon had emerged above the trees on the opposite side of the river. It struck and illumined something white above me. I was standing exactly where I had stood on that fatal tenth of August, so many years before.

I came to my senses as if by an electric shock.

At last everything was clear to me. At last I understood whence had gone all my vanity and jealousy. At last I understood the spell of peace that had settled on me in that moonlit tenth of August, in that far off city.

My burden had passed through the Valley of the Shadow of Death with her--for I was standing at the door of her tomb!

I did not question. I knew, I comprehended.

In no other way could I have found such calm.

Though I flung myself on the shining marble steps that led in the moonlight up to the top of the knoll where the tomb stood, I had no tears to shed.

The present floated still further away.

Even the rush of the torrent died out of my ears.

Once more it seemed to me that lovely day in May when we three had marched, shoulder to shoulder, down the city street--that spring day in the early sixties, when the North was sending her flower to fight for a united country.

Again I felt the warm sunshine on my head.

Once more I heard the ringing cheers, saw the floating flags, and the faces of women who wept as well as women who smiled in the throngs that lined the street.

Just as in all my life it had been his emotions and his enthusiasms that led me, it was his excitement that impelled me forward at this moment. His was the hand that in my school days, at college, in our Bohemian days abroad, had swept my responsive nature as a master hand strikes a harp, and made harmonies or discords at his will--or, I should say, according to his mood.

I used to think in those days that he never willfully wronged any one, but I had to own also that he never deliberately sacrificed himself for any one. And, if I were the victim of his temperament, he was no less so. But he was an artist. I was not. All things either good or bad were merely material to him. With me it was different.

He and I were alone in the world. But beside us marched, that May morning, with the glory of youth on his handsome but weak face, one whose "baptism of fire" was to make him a hero, who had else been remembered a coward.

The story of the girl he had wronged, and fear of whom had even reconciled his family to his enlisting, was common property, and had been for several seasons. There was a child, too, a little daughter, fondly loved, but unacknowledged, the fame of whose childish beauty many a heedless voice had already sung.

He, poor youngster, looked on his all that morning.

Once more I saw the flag draped house where his mother waved a brave farewell to him.

But there was another later picture in my mind. Again I heard the blare of the band before us as it flung its satire of "The Girl I Left Behind Me," into the spring air. I saw once more in my mind the child, with her floating red gold curls, raised above the crowd on the shoulders of tall men. Her eyes were too young for tears--and for that matter, tears came to her but seldom in later years--and the lips that shouted "bood-bye" smiled, unconscious of bravery, as she swung her hat with its symbolic colors above her shining head.

That was the picture that three of us carried to the front.

We left him--all his errors redeemed by a noble death--with his face turned up to the stars, as silent, as mysterious as they, after our first battle.

From the horrors of that night we two came away bound by an oath to care for that child.

*   *   *   *   *

Again my memory shifted to the days that found her a woman. Fair, beautiful, dainty, her father's daughter in looks, but inheriting from a rare mother a peculiar strength of character, a moral force rarely found with such a temperament and such beauty.

We had aided to raise her as became the child of her father, whose story she knew as soon as she was able to understand, but she knew it from the lips of the brave mother, who cherished his memory. Until she was a woman grown it was I, however, who, of her two self-appointed guardians, had watched over her. Children did not interest him.

He had married some years before that time, married well with an eye to a calm comfortable future, as became an artist who could not be hampered by the need of money.

Indeed, it was not until he knew that I was to marry her that he really looked at her.

And I, with all my experience of him, simply because I was never able to understand the dual nature, failed at that fatal hour when we stood together beside our protegee to apply to the situation the knowledge that years of experience should have taught me.

I was so bound up in my own feelings that I failed to remember that, until then, I had never had a great emotion that his nature had not acted as a lens in the kindling.

Then, too, there was a dense sense of the conventional--a logical enough birthright--in my make-up. I, who had known him so long, so well, seemed, nevertheless, when he married, to have fancied there was some hocus-pocus in the ceremony, which should make a definite change in a man's character, as well as a presumable change in his way of life.

It must have been that there, in the open, at the foot of the knoll, I slept, as one does the first night after a long awaited death, when the relief that pain is passed, and suspense ended, deadens grief. She was no longer in this world of torture. That helped me.

*   *   *   *   *

The next I knew, it was the sun, and not the moon which was shining on me.
The wind had stilled its sobbing in the trees.
Only the rushing of the river sounded in my ears.
I rose slowly, and mounted the steps.
A tiny white marble mosque of wonderful beauty--for he who erected it was one of the world's great artists, whose works will live to glorify his name and his art

when all his follies shall have been forgotten--stood in a court paved with marble.

It was encircled with a low coping of the whitest of stone. Over this low wall vines were already growing, and the woodbine that was mingled with it was stained with those glorious tints in which Nature says to life, "Even death is beautiful."

The wide bronze doors on either side were open.

I accepted the fact without even wondering why--or asking myself who, in opening them, had discovered my presence!

I entered.

For a brief time I stood once more within the room where she lay.

An awful peace fell on my soul, as if her soul had whispered in the words we had so often read together:

"I lie so composedly   Now in my bed--"

I knew at last, as I gazed, that all her life, and all mine, as well, had been to his profit. That out of this, too, he had wrought some of his greatness.

The interior of the vault was of red marble, and, such of chiselling as there was done, seemed wonderful to me even in my frame of mind. I took it all in, through unwilling, though fascinated eyes.

I have never seen it since. I can never forget it.

Yet art is, and always has been, so much to me, that I could not help, even in my strangely wrought-up mental condition, comprehending and admiring his scheme and the masterly manner in which he had worked it out.

At my feet, as I stood on the threshold, was an elaborate scroll engraved on the stone and surrounded with a wreath of leaves, that vied with the tombs of the old world. As I gazed at it, and read the gothic letters in which it was set forth that this monument was erected in adoration of this woman, how well I remembered the day when we had crouched together over those stones in the crypt at Certosa, to admire the chiselling of Donatello which had inspired this.

There was a space left for the signature of the artist, which would, I knew, some day be written there boldly enough!

In the centre stood the sarcophagus.

I felt its presence, though my eyes avoided it.

Above, on the wall, were the words borne along by carved angels:

"My love she sleeps: Oh, may her sleep   As it was lasting, so be deep."

And I seemed to hear her voice intone the words as I had heard them from her lips so many times.

And then my eyes fell--on her! Aye! On her, stretched at full length in her warm and glorious tomb. For above her mortal remains slept her effigy wrought with all the skill of a great art.

I had feared to look upon it, but having looked, I felt that I could never tear myself away from its peace and loveliness.

The long folds of the drapery fell straight from the small, round throat to the tiny unshod feet, and so wonderfully was it wrought, that it seemed as if the living beautiful flesh of the slender body was still quick beneath it. The exquisite hands that I knew so well--so delicate, and yet so strong--were gently crossed upon her breast, and her arms held a long stemmed lily, emblem of purity, and it looked to me there like a martyr's palm.

Perhaps it was the pale reflection from the red walls, but the figure seemed too real to be mere stone!

I forgot the irony of the fact that I was merely seeing her through his eyes--the eyes of the man who had robbed me. I felt only her presence. I fell on my knees. I flung my arms across the beautiful form--no colder to my embrace than had been the living woman! As I recoiled from the death-like touch, my eyes fell on the words carved on the face of the sarcophagus, and once more, it was like the voice that was hushed in my ears.

> "I pray to God that she may lie
> Forever with unopened eye
> While the dim sheeted ghosts go by."

"Amen," I said, with all my heart, to the words he had carved above her, for what, after the fever of such a life, could be so welcome to her as dreamless, eternal silence, in which there would be no more passion, no more struggling, no more love?

And, if I wished with all my soul, that the great surprise of death might, for her, have been peace and silence, did I not bar myself as well as him from the hope of Heaven?

How long I stood there, with hungry eyes devouring the marble effigy of her I so loved--now tortured by its fidelity, now punished by its coldness--I never knew.

Sometimes I noticed the changing of the light, the shifting of the shadows, as the sun swung steadily upward, but it was a subconscious observation which did not recall me to myself and the present.

Back, back turned my thoughts to the past.

Here, where she now lay in her gorgeous tomb, had then stood an arbor, and below had roared the rushing river.

It was the night of our wedding.

Then, as now, on this very spot, I had looked down on that fair pale face, and then it had given me back a gaze as lifeless as this.

I had missed my bride from the little throng in the quaint house beyond. I had stolen out to seek her. Instinctively I had turned to the old arbor above the river, where her hours of meditation had always been passed.

It was there I had found her as a child, when I came to bring her father's dying message. It was there I had asked her to become my wife. It was there we three had first stood together.

For a week before the wedding she had been in a strange mood, tearless, but nervous, and sad! Still, it had not seemed to me an unnatural mood in such a woman, on the eve of her marriage.

Fate is ironical.

I remembered that I was serenely happy as I sped up the hill in search of her, and so sure that I knew where to find her. Light scudding clouds crossed the track of the moon, which, with a broadly smiling face, rolled up the heavens at a spinning pace, now appearing, now disappearing behind the flying clouds.

I was humming gaily as I strode along the narrow path. Nothing tugged at my heart strings to warn me of approaching sorrow. There was no signal in all nature to prepare me for the end in a complete shipwreck of all my dreams. The peace about me gave no hint of its cynicism. Nothing, either within or without, hinted that my hours of happiness and content were running out rapidly to the last sand!

I had reached the shallow steps that led up the knoll to the arbor!

At that moment the clouds were swept off from the face of the moon, and the white light fell full on her.

But she was not alone. She rested in the arms of my friend, as, God help me, she had never rested in mine--in an abandon that was only too eloquent.

What was said?

Who but God knows that now?

What do men like us, who have thought themselves one in all things, until one love rends them asunder, say at such a time? As for me, I cannot recall a word!

I did not even see his face.

I think he saw mine no more.

We seemed to see into the soul of each other, through the very heart of that frail woman between us, that slender creature in the bridal dress, who sank down before us, as if the colliding passions of two strong men had killed her.

It was he who raised her up. His hands placed her in my arms. No need to say that she was blameless. I knew all that.

It was only Fate after all, that I blamed, yet the fatalist is human. He suffers in living like other men--sometimes more, because he refuses to struggle in the clutches of Chance!

As I gazed down into her white face, I heard the steps of my friend, even above the roaring of the river, as he strode down the hillside, out of my life! And I know not even to-day which was the bitterest grief, the loss of my faith in being loved, or the passing from my heart of that man!

Of the pain of the night that followed, only the silence and our own hearts knew.

Love and passion are so twinned in some hours of life that one cannot distinguish in himself the one from the other.

Into my keeping "to have and to hold," the law had given this beautiful woman, "until death should us part." I loved her! But, out of her heart, at once stronger and weaker than mine, my friend had barred me.

It is not in hours like these, that all men can be sane.

I thought of what might have been, if they had not met that night, and my ignoble side craved ignorance of that Chance, or the brutality to ignore it.

I looked down into that cold face as I laid her from the arms that had borne her down the hill--laid her on what was to have been her nuptial couch--and closed the door between us and all the world.

We were together--alone--at last!

I had dreamed of this hour. Here was its realization. I watched the misery of remembrance dawn slowly on her white face. I pitied her as I gazed at her, yet my whole being cried out in rage at its own pity. On her trembling lips I seemed to see his kisses. In her frightened eyes I saw his image. The shudder that shook her whole body as her eyes held mine, confessed him--and that confession kept me at bay.

All that night I sat beside her.

What mad words I uttered a merciful nature never let me recall.

In the chill dawn I fled from her presence.

The width of the world had lain between us, me--and this woman whom I had worshipped, of whom a consuming jealousy had made ten years of my life a mad fever, which only her death had cured. Saner men have protested against the same situation that ruined me--and yet, even in my reasoning moments, like this, I knew that to have rebelled would have been to have forced a tragic climax before the hour at which Fate had fixed it.

*   *   *   *   *

When something--I know not what--recalled me again to the present, I found that I had sat by her a day, as, on our last meeting, I watched out the night. The sun, which had sent its almost level rays in at the east door of the tomb when I entered, was now shining in brilliant almost level rays in at the west.

The day was passing.

A shadow fell from the opposite door. I became suddenly conscious of his presence, and, once more, across her body, I looked into my friend's eyes.

Between us, as on that dreadful night, she was stretched!

But she was at peace.

Our colliding emotions might rend us, they could never again tear at her gentle heart. That was at rest.

Over her we stood once more, as if years had not passed--years of silence.

Above the woman we had both loved, we two, who had stood shoulder to shoulder in battle, been one in thought and ambition until passion rent us asunder, met as we parted, but she was at peace!

We had severed without farewells.

We met without greetings.

We stood in silence until he waved me to a broad seat behind me, and sank into a similar niche opposite.

We sat in the shadow.

She lay between us in the level light of the setting sun, which fell across her from the wide portal, and once more our eyes met on her face, but they would not disturb her calm.

His influence was once more upon me.

In the silence--for it was some time before he spoke, and I was dumb--my ac-cursed eye for detail had taken in the change in him. Yet I fancied I was not looking at him. I noted that he had aged--that this was one of the periods in him which I knew so well--when a passion for work was on him, and the fever and fervor of creation trained him down like a race-horse, all spirit and force. I noted that he still wore the velveteens and the broad hat and loose open collar of his student days.

Sitting on either side of the tomb he had built to enshrine her, on carved mar-ble seats such as Tuscan poets sat on, in the old days, to sing to fair women, with our gaze focussed on the long white form between us--ah, between us indeed!--his voice broke the long silence.

He leaned forward, his elbows on his knees, and the broad brim of his soft hat swept the marble floor with a gentle rhythmic swish, as it swung idly from his loos-ened grasp. I heard it as an accompaniment to his voice.

His eyes never once strayed from her face.

"You think you are to be pitied," he said. "You are wrong! No one who has not sinned against another needs pity. I meant you no harm. Fate--my temperament, your immobility, the very gifts that have made me what I am were to blame--if blame there were. Every one of us must live out his life, according to his nature. I, as well as you!

"When, on this very spot where we last parted, you told me that you loved her, I swear to you, if need be, that I rejoiced. I was glad that she would have you to make the future smooth for her. Later I grew to envy you. It was for your safety, as well as mine and hers, that I decided to see neither of you again until she had been some time your wife. No word of love, no confidence of any kind, had ever passed between us. When I wrote you that I should not be here to see you married, and when not even your reproaches could move me, I had already engaged my passage on a sailing ship bound for the Azores. I had planned to put a long uncertain voyage between you and any possibility that I might mar your chances for happiness, for the nearer the day came, the more--in spite of myself--I resented it!

"My good intentions were thwarted by--Fate.

"For some reason, forgotten and unimportant, the Captain deferred lifting anchor for a whole week. I called myself unpretty names for thinking that I could not even see her without danger. I despised myself for the judgment that accused me of being such a scamp as to think I would do anything to rob her of the protection and safety you could give her, and I could not, and an egoist for being possessed with the idea that I could if I would.

"Suddenly I felt quite sure of myself.

"Yet I had meant to see her without being seen, when I hurried so unexpectedly down here on your wedding night. I fancied I only longed to see what a lovely bride she would make--she who as a child, a girl, a maiden, had been in your eyes the most exquisite creature you had ever known; she whom I had avoided for years, because I, of all men, could least afford to take a place in her life! I longed to see those eyes, still so pure, under her bridal veil.

"I came in secret! I saw her--and all prudence fled out of me, leaving but one instinct.

"Was it my fault that, alone, she fled from the house? That, with her veil thrown over her arm, she ran directly by me, like a sprite in the moonlight, to this spot?

"The rest you know.

"It is not you who need pity!

"You have the pain of an imperishable loyalty in your soul. It is like a glory in your face, in spite of all you have suffered. As I look at you, it seems but yesterday that all was well between us.

"I lost much in losing you.

"Nor am I sure that you were right to go! But that was for your own nature to decide. In your place I should have fought Fate, I expected you to do it.

"I loved her first, because she satisfied my eyes. I loved her the more that she was denied to me! Yet I knew always that this love was not in me what it was in you. With me it was, like many other emotions of a similar sort--a sentiment that would pass. I tried to think otherwise. But I had awakened her heart, and you, to whom the law had given her, were gone!

"I waited long for your return, or for some sign.

"You neither came nor spoke.

"I argued that something must be done. I owed it to her to offer her my protection.

"I came back here. I met her on this very spot. I said to her, 'You are alone in the world--your mother has married--she has other children. I have saddened your life with my love. Let me at least help to cheer it again. You need affection. Here it is--in my arms!'

"And, while I waited for her answer, I prayed with all my soul that she might deny me.

"God bless her! She did! I turned away from her with a glad heart, and in that heart I enshrined this woman, who, loving me, had denied me. There I set up her image, pure and inviolate. Two long years I stayed away from her, and as I worked, I worshipped her, and out of that worship I wrought a great thing.

"With time, however, her real image grew faint within me. Other emotions, other experiences seemed to blur and dim it. In spite of myself, I returned here. Once more I stood on this spot, within the gaze of her deep eyes. I began to believe that a love everlasting, all enduring, had been given me! But still it was passion that pleaded for possession, and still it was self-knowledge that looked on in fear.

"Passion bade me plead: 'You love me! You need me! Come to me!' And fear kept my heart still, in dread of her consent.

"But she looked up into my face with eyes that seemed to widen under mine, and simply whispered, 'My mother.' The heart that knew and understood now all that sad history seemed to feel that her act might re-open the mother's old wound; that the verdict 'like mother, like daughter' would turn virtue back to sin again.

"Once more I went out into the world with a light heart! Her virtue, her strength, seemed to be mine. I went back to my work with renewed spirit, back to my life with no new self-reproach.

"But once more I swung round the circle. With a perversity that, dreading success, and conscious of fear, yet longs to strive for what it dreads to win, I returned to her again. The death of her mother was my new excuse.

"She came to me--here, as usual. But this time she came leading by the hand her little sister, and I felt her armored against me even before I spoke.

"You, who used to believe in a merciful God, can you explain to me why he has left in the nature of man, created--so you believe--in His own image--that impulse to destroy that which he loves? I loved her for exactly what she was. I loved her because she had the courage to resist me. Yet from each denial so ardently desired, so thankfully received, my soul sprang up strengthened in desire. Safe above me I worshipped her. Once in my arms, I knew, only too well, that even that love would pass as all other emotions had done. I knew I should put her aside, gently if I could, urgently, if I must, and pass on. That is my Fate! Everything that enters my life leaves something I need--and departs! For what I have not, I hunger. What I win soon wearies me. It is the price life exacts for what it gives me.

"So, when August of this year came round, I found myself once more standing here.

"Ten years had passed since we stood here with her between us--ten years that had laid their richest gifts on her beauty. This time she was indeed alone. As I looked into her face, I somehow thought of Agamemnon's fair daughter doomed to die a virgin. You can see my 'Iphigenia' in the spring, if you chance to be in Paris.

"This time, self-knowledge deserted me. The past was forgotten. The future was undreaded. The passion in my heart spoke without reserve or caution! I no longer said: 'You need me! You love me!' I cried out: 'I can no longer live without you!' I no longer said, 'Come to me!' I pleaded, 'Take me to your heart. There, where my image is, let me rest at last. I have waited long, be kind to me.'

"I saw her sway toward me as once before she had done. It was too late to look backward or forward. I had conquered. In my weakness I believed it was thus ordained--that I deserved some credit for waiting so long.

"Yet, when she left me here alone, having promised, with downcast eyes that avoided mine, to place her hand in mine, and walk boldly beside me down the forbidden path of the world, I fell down on the spot her feet had pressed, and wept bitterly, as I had never done before in all my life. Wept over the shattered ideal, the faith I had so wilfully torn down, the miserable victory of my meanest self.

"I thought the end was come. Fate was merciful to me, however!

"I had myself fixed the following Thursday as the day for our departure. As I dated a letter to her that night my mind involuntarily reckoned the days, and I was startled to find that Thursday fell on that fatal tenth of August.

"I had not thought I could be so tortured in my mind as I was by the dread that she should notice the dire coincidence.

"She did!

"The hour that should have brought her to me, brought a note instead. It was dated boldly 'August tenth.' It was without beginning or signature. It said--I can repeat every word--'Of the two roads to self-destruction open to me, I have chosen the one that will, in the end, give the least pain to you. I love you. I have always loved you since I was a child. I do not regret anything yet! Thank God for me that I depart without ever having seen a look of weariness in the eyes that gazed so lovingly into mine when we parted, and thank Him for yourself that you will never see a look of reproach in mine. I know no time so fitting to say a long farewell for both of us as this--Farewell, then.'

"I knew what I should find when I went up the hill.

"The doctors said 'heart disease.' She had been troubled with some such weakness. I alone knew the truth! As I had known myself, she had known me!

"You think you suffer--you, who might, but for me, have made her happy, as such women should be, in a world of simple natural joys! My friend, loss without guilt is pain--but it is not without the balm of virtuous compensation. You have at least a right to grieve.

"But I! I am forced to know myself. To feel myself borne along in spite of myself; and to realize that she who should have worn a crown of happy womanhood, lies there a sacrifice, to be bewailed like Jepthah's one fair daughter; and to sit here in full dread of the ebbing of even this great emotion, knowing too well that it will pass out of my life when it shall have achieved its purpose, leaving only as evidence *this*--another great work, crystalized into immortality in everlasting stone. I know that I cannot long hold it here in my heart. The day will come--perhaps soon--when I shall stand outside that door, and recognize this as my work, and be proud of it, without the power to grieve, as I do now; when I shall approve my own handiwork, and be unable to mourn for her who was sacrificed to achieve it. What is your pain to mine?"

And I saw the hot tears drop from his eyes. I saw them fall on the marble floor, and they watered the very spot where his name was so soon to spring up in pride to confess his handiwork.

I looked on her calm face. I knew she did not regret her part! I rose, and, without a word, I passed out at the wide door, and, without looking back, I passed down the slope in the dusk, and left them together--the woman I had loved, and the friend I had lost!

*   *   *   *   *

As his voice died away, he sat upright quickly, threw a glance about the circle, and, with another fine gesture said: "Et voila!"

The Doctor was the only one to really laugh, though a broad grin ran round the circle.

"Well," remarked the Doctor, who had been leaning against a tree, and indulging in shrugs and an occasional groan, which had not even disconcerted the story teller, "I suppose that is how that very great man, your governor, did the trick. I can see him in every word."

"That is all you know about it," laughed the Sculptor. "That is not a bit how the governor did it. That is how I should have done it, had I been the governor, and had the old man's chances. I call that an ideal thing to happen to a man."

"Not even founded on fact--which might have been some excuse for telling it," groaned the Critic. "I'd love to write a review of that story. I'd polish it off."

"Of course you would," sneered the Sculptor. "That's all a critic is for--to polish off the tales he can't write. I call that a nice romantic, ideal tale for a sculptor to conceive, and as the Doctor said the other night, it is a possible story, since I conceived it, and what the mind of mortal can conceive, can happen."

"The trouble," said the Journalist, "with chaps like you, and the Critic, is that your people are all framework. They're not a bit of flesh and blood."

"I'd like to know," said the Sculptor, throwing himself back in his chair, "who has a right to decide that?"

"What I'd like to know," said the Youngster, "is, what did she do between times? Of course he sculpted, and earned slathers of money. But she--?"

"Oh, ouch--help!" cried the Sculptor. "Do I know?"

"Exactly!" answered the Critic, "and that you don't sticks out in every line of your story."

"Goodness me, you might ask the same thing about Leda, or Helen of Troy."

"Ha! Ha!" laughed the Doctor. "But we know what they did!"

"A lot you do. It is because they are old classics, and you accept them, whereas my story is quite new and original--and you were unprepared for it, and so you can't appreciate it. Anyway, it's my first-born story, and I'll defend it with my life."

Only a laugh replied to the challenge, and the attitude of defense he struck, as he leaped to his feet, though the Journalist said, under his breath, "It takes a carver in stone to think of a tale like that!"

"But think," replied the Doctor, "how much trouble some women would escape if they kept on saying A B C like that--for the A B C is usually lovely--and when it was time to X Y Z--often terrible, they just slipped out through the 'open door.'"

"On the other hand, they *risk* losing heaps of fun," said the Journalist.

"What I like about that story," said the Lawyer, "is that it is so aristocratic. Every one seems to have plenty of money. They all three do just what they like, have no duties but to analyze themselves, and evidently everything goes like clockwork. The husband enjoys being morbid, and has the means to be gloriously so. The sculptor likes to carve Edgar Allan Poe all over the place, and the fair lady is able to gratify the tastes of both men."

"You can laugh as much as you please," sighed the Sculptor, "I wish it had happened to me."

"Well," said the Doctor, "you have the privilege of going to bed and dreaming that it did."

"Thank you," answered the Sculptor. "That is just what I am going to do."

"What did I tell you last night?" said the Doctor, under his breath, as he watched the Sculptor going slowly toward the house. "Bet he has been telling that tale to himself under many skies for years!"

"I suppose," laughed the Journalist, "that the only reason he has never built the tomb is that he has never had the money."

"Oh, be fair!" said the Violinist. "He has not built the tomb because he is not his father. The old man would have done it in a minute, only he lacked imagination. You bet he never day-dreamed, and yet what skill he had, and what adventures! He never saw anything but the facts of life, yet how magnificently he recorded them."

"It is a pity," sighed the Violinist, "that the son did not seek a different career."

"What difference does it make after all?" remarked the Doctor. "One never knows when the next generation will step up or down, and, after all, what does it matter?"

"It is all very well for you to talk," said the Critic.

"I assure you that the great pageant would have been just as interesting from any other point of view. It has been a great spectacle,--this living. I'm glad I've seen it."

"Amen to that," said the Divorcee. "I only hope I am going to see it again--even though it hurts."

VI

THE DIVORCEE'S STORY
ONE WOMAN'S PHILOSOPHY
THE TALE OF A MODERN WIFE

As I look back, I remember that the next night was one of the most trying of the week.

As we came down to dinner we all had visions of the destruction of Louvain, and the burning of the famous library. It is hard enough to think of lives going out; still, as the Doctor was so fond of saying, "man is born to die, and woman, too," but that the great works of men, his bequest to the coming generations, should be wantonly destroyed, seemed even more horrible, especially to those who love beauty, and the idea of the charred leaves of the library flying in the air above the historic city of catholic culture, made us all feel as if we were sitting down to a funeral service rather than a very good dinner.

Matters were not made any gayer because Angele, who was waiting on table, had rings round her eyes, which told of sleepless nights. And why? We were mere spectators. We had been interested to dispute and look on. But she knew that somewhere out there in the northeast her man was carrying a gun.

Yet all about us the country was so lovely and so tranquil, horses were walking the fields, and, even as we sat at dinner, we could hear the voices and the heavy feet of the peasant women as they went home from their work. The garden had never been more beautiful than it was that evening, with the silver light of the moon through the trees, and the smell of the freshly watered earth and flowers.

We had no doubt who was to contribute the story. The Divorcee was dressed with unusual care for the role, and carried a big lace bag on her arm, and, as she leaned back in her chair, she pulled one of the big old fashioned candles in its deep glass toward her, and said with a nervous laugh:

"I shall have to ask you to let me read my story. You know I am not accustomed to this sort of thing. It is really my very 'first appearance,' and I could not possibly tell it as the rest of you more experienced people can do," and she took the manuscript out of her lace bag, and, settling herself gracefully, unrolled it. The Youngster put a stool under her pretty feet, and the Doctor set a cushion behind her back, while the Journalist, with a laugh, poured her a glass of water, and the Violinist ceremoniously leaned over, and asked, "Shall I turn for you?"

She could not help laughing, but it did not make her any the less nervous, or her voice any the less shaky as she began:

$$* \qquad * \qquad * \qquad * \qquad *$$

It was after dinner on one of those rare occasions when they dined alone together.

They were taking coffee in Mrs. Shattuck's especial corner of the drawing-room, and she had just asked her husband to smoke.

She was leaning back comfortably in a nest of cushions, in her very latest gown, with a most becoming light falling on her from the tall, yellow-shaded lamp.

He was facing her--astride his chair, in a position man has loved since creation.

He was just thinking that his wife had never looked handsomer, finer, in fact, in all her life--quite the satisfactory, all-round, desirable sort of a woman a man's wife ought to be.

She was wondering if he would ever be any less attractive to all women than he was now at forty-two--or any better able to resist his own power.

As she put her coffee cup back on the tiny table at her elbow, he leaned forward, and picked up a book which lay open on a chair near him, and carelessly glanced at it.

"Schopenhauer," and he wrinkled his brows and glanced half whimsically down the page. "I never can get used to a woman reading that stuff--and in French, at that. If you took it up to perfect your German there would be some sense in it."

Mrs. Shattuck did not reply. When a moment later, she did speak it was to ignore his remark utterly, and ask:

"The *Kaiser Wilhelm* got off in good season this morning--speaking of German things?"

"Oh, yes," was the indifferent reply, "at ten o'clock, quite promptly."

"I suppose she was comfortable, and that you explained why I could not come?"

"Certainly. One of your beastly head-aches. She understood."

"Thank you."

Shattuck yawned lazily, and changed the subject, which did not seem to interest him.

"Do you mean to say," he asked, still turning the leaves of the book he held, "that this pleases you?"

"Not exactly."

"Well, amuses you? Instructs you, if you like that better?"

"No, I mean to say simply--since you insist--that he speaks the truth, and there are some--even among women--who must know the truth and abide by it."

"Well, thank Heaven," said the man, pulling at his cigar, "that most women are more emotional than intelligent--as Nature meant them to be."

Mrs. Shattuck examined her daintily polished nails, rubbed them carefully on the palm of her hand, as women have a trick of doing, and then polished them on her lace handkerchief, before she said, "Yes, it is a pity that we are not all like that,--a very great pity--for our own sakes. Yet, unluckily, some of us *will* think."

"But the thinking woman is so rarely logical, so unable to take life impersonally, that Schopenhauer does her no good. He only fills her mind with errors, mistrust, unhappiness."

"You men always argue that way with women--as if life were not the same for us as for you. Pass me the book. I wager that I can open it at random, and that you cannot deny the truth of the first sentence I read."

He passed her the book.

She took it, laid it open carelessly on her knees, bending the covers far back that it might stay open, and she gave her finger tips a final rub with her handkerchief before she looked at the page. She paused a bit after she glanced at it, then picked up the book and read: "'L'homme est par Nature porte a l'inconstance dans l'amour, la femme a la fidelite. L'amour de l'homme baisse d'une facon sensible a partir de l'instant ou il a obtenu satisfaction: il semble que toute autre femme ait plus d'attrait que celle qu'il possede.'"

She laid the book down, but she did not look at him.

"Rubbish," was his remark.

"Yes, I know. You men always find it so easy to say 'rubbish' to all natural truths which you prefer not to discuss."

"Well, my dear Naomi, it seems to me that if you are to advocate Schopenhauer, you must go the whole length with him. The fault is in Nature, and you must accept it as inevitable, and not kick against it."

"I don't kick against Nature--as you put it--I kick against civilization, which makes laws regardless of Nature, which deliberately shuts its eyes to all natural truths in regard to the relations of men to women,--and is therefore forced to continually wink to avoid confessing its folly."

"Civilization seems to me to have done the best it could with a very difficult problem. It has not actually allowed different codes of morals to men and women, and it may have had to wink on that account. Right there, in your Schopenhauer, you have a primal reason, that is, if you chose to follow your philosopher to the extent of actually believing that Nature has deliberately, from the beginning, protected women against that sin of which so much is made, and to which she has, as deliberately, for economic reasons of her own, tempted men."

"I do believe it, truly."

"You are no more charitable toward my sex than most women are. Yet neither your teacher nor you may be right. A theoretic arguer like Schopenhauer makes good enough reading for calm minds, but he is bad for an emotional temperament, and, by Jove, Naomi, he was a bad example of his own philosophy."

"My dear Dick, I am afraid I read Schopenhauer because I thought what he writes long before I ever heard of him. I read him because did I not find a clear logical mind going the same way my mind will go, I might be troubled with doubts, and afraid that I was going quite wrong."

"Well, the deuce and all with a woman when she begins to read stuff like that is her inability to generalize. You women take everything home to yourselves. You try to deduct conclusions from your own lives which men like Schopenhauer have scanned the centuries for. The natural course of your life could hardly have provided you with the pessimism with which--I hope you will pardon my remark, my dear--you have treated me several times in the past few months. Chamfort and Schopenhauer did that. But these are not subjects a man discusses easily with his wife."

"Indeed? Then that is surely an error of civilization. If a man can discuss such matters more easily with a woman who is not his wife, it is because there is no frankness in marriage. Dick, did it ever occur to you that a man and woman, strongly attracted toward one another, might live together many years without understanding each other?"

"God forbid!"

"How easily you say that!"

"I have heard that most women think they are not understood, but I never reflected on the matter."

"You and I have not troubled one another much with our doubts and perplexities."

"You and I have been very happy together--I hope." There was a little pause before the last two words, as if he had expected her to anticipate them with something, and there was a half interrogative note in his voice. She made no response, so he went on, "I've surely not been a hard master--and I hope I've not been selfish. I know I've not been unloving."

"And I hope you've not suffered many discomforts on my account. I think, as women go, I am fairly reasonable--or I have been."

For some reason Shattuck seemed to find the cigar he was smoking most unsatisfactory. Either it had been broken, or he had unconsciously chewed the end--a thing which he detested--and there was a pause while he discarded the weed, and selected a fresh one. He appeared to be reflecting as he lighted it, and if his mind could have been read, it would have probably been discovered that he was wondering how it had happened that the conversation had taken this turn, and mentally cursing his own stupidity in making any remarks on the Schopenhauer. He was conscious all the time that his wife was looking rather steadily at him, and he knew that at least a conventional reply was expected of him.

"My dear girl," he said, "I look back on ten very satisfactory years of married life. You have been a model wife, a charming companion--and if occasionally it has occurred to me--just lately--that my wife has developed rather singular, to say the least, unflattering ideas of life, why, you have such a brilliant way of putting it, that I am more than half proud that you've the brains to hold such ideas, though they are a bit disconcerting to me as a husband. I suppose the development is logical enough. You were always, even as a girl, inclined to making footnotes. I suppose their present daring is simply the result of our being just a little older than we used to be. I suppose if we did not outgrow our illusions, the road to death would be too tragic."

For a moment she made no reply. Then, as if for the first time owning to the idea which had long been uppermost in her mind, she said suddenly: "The truth of the matter is, that I really believe marriage is foolish. I do believe that no man ever approached it without regretting that civilization had made it necessary, and that many men would escape, at the very last moment, if women did not so rigidly hold them to their promises, and if, between two ridiculous positions, marriage having been pushed nearest, had not become desperately inevitable."

"How absurd, Naomi, when you see the whole procession of men walking,--according to their dispositions--calmly or eagerly to their fate every day."

"Nevertheless, I think the pre-nuptial confessions of a majority of men of our class, would prove that what I say is true."

"Are you hinting that it was true in your case?"

"Perhaps."

Shattuck gave an amused laugh. "Do you mean to say that you kept me to the point?"

"Not exactly. At that time I had an able bodied father who would have had to be dealt with. Besides, a man does not own up even to himself--not always--when he finds himself face to face with the inevitable. I am not speaking of what men talk about in such cases, or of what they do, but of what they feel,--of the fact that, in too many instances, Nature not having meant men for bondage, after they have passed the Rubicon to that spot from which the code of civilized honor does not permit them to turn back, they usually have a period of regret, and are forced to make a real effort to face the Future,--to go on, in fact."

The smile had died out of Shattuck's face and he said quite seriously: "As far as we are concerned, Naomi, I have very different recollections of the whole affair."

"Have you? And yet, months before we were married, I knew that it would not have broken your heart if the wedding had not come off at all."

"My dear, the modern heart does not break easily in this age. We are schooled to meet the accidents of life with some philosophy."

"And yet to have lost you then, would have killed me."

Shattuck looked at her sharply, with, one might almost have said, a new interest, but she was no longer looking at him. She went on, hurriedly: "You loved me, of course. I was of your world. I was a woman that other men liked, and therefore a desirable woman. I was of good family--altogether your social equal, in fact, quite the sort of woman it became you to marry. I pleased you--and I loved you."

"Thank you, my dear," he said. "In ten years, I doubt if you have ever made so frank a declaration as that--in words." He was wondering, if, after all, she were going to develop into an emotional woman, and his heart gave a quick leap at the very thought--for there are hours when a woman who runs too much to head has a man at a cruel disadvantage.

"Things are so much harder, so much more complex for a woman," she went on.

"For the protection of the community?"

"Perhaps. Still, it is not always pleasant to be a woman,--and yet think; a woman whose reason has been mistakenly developed at the expense of her capacity to enjoy being a woman, and who is forced at the same time to encounter the laws of Nature, and pay at the same time, the penalty of being a woman, and the penalty of knowledge. For, just so surely as we live, we must encounter love.--"

"You might take it out," interrupted the husband, "in feeling flattered that it takes so much to conquer such as you."

"So we might, but that, once conquered, neither man nor Nature has any further use for us, and regret, like art, is long. Not even you can deny," she exclaimed, sitting up in some excitement, and letting her cushions fall in a mess all about her, "that life is very unfair to women."

"Well, I don't see that. Physically it is a little rough on you, but there are compensations."

"I have never been able to discover them. Love itself is hard on a woman. It seems to stir a man's faculties healthily. They seem the stronger and more fit for it. It does not seem to uproot a man's whole being. Does it serve women in that way?"

"I bear witness that it makes some of you deucedly handsome. And I have heard that it makes some of you--good."

"Yes, as chastisement does. No, Life seems to have adjusted matters between men and women very badly, very unjustly."

"And yet, as this life is the only one we know we must adjust ourselves to it as we find it."

"No, no. We had better have accepted the thing as Nature gave it to us. We came into this world like beasts--why aren't we content to live like beasts, and make no pretenses? Women would have nothing to expect then, and there'd be no such thing as broken hearts. In spite of all the polish of civilization, man is simply bent on conquest. Woman is only one phase of the chase to him--a chase in which every active virile man is occupied from his cradle to his grave. You are the conquerors. We are simply the conquered."

Shattuck tried to make his voice light, as he said: "Not always unhappy ones, I fancy."

"I suppose all men flatter themselves that way, and argue that probably the Sabine women preferred their fate to no fate at all."

"Don't be bitter on so old and impersonal a topic, Naomi. It is the law of life that one must give, and one must take. That the emotions differ does not prove that one is better than the other."

Shattuck took a turn up and down the long room, not quite at ease with himself.

Mrs. Shattuck seemed to be thinking. As he passed her, he stopped, picked up her cushions, and re-arranged them about her, with an idle caress by the way, a kiss gently dropped on the inside of her white wrist.

She followed his every movement with a strange speculative look in her eyes, almost as if he were some new and strange animal that she was studying for the first time.

When she spoke again, it was to go on as if she had not been interrupted, "It seems to me that man comes out of a great passion just as good as new, while a woman is shattered--in a moral sense--and never fully recovers herself."

Shattuck's back was toward her when he replied. "Sorry to spoil any more illusions, dear child, but how about the long list of men who are annually ruined by it? The men in the prisons, the men who kill themselves, the men who hang for it?"

"Those are crimes. I am not talking of the criminal classes, but of the world in which normal people live."

"Our set," he laughed, "but that is not the whole world, alas!"

"I know that men--well bred, cultivated, refined, even honorable men,--seem to be able to repeat every emotion of life. A woman scales the heights but once. Hence it must depend, in the case of women capable of deep love--on the men whether the relation into which marriage betrays them be decent or indecent. What I should like to be able to discover is--what provision does either man or civilization propose to make for the woman whom Fate, in wanton irony, reduces, even in marriage, to the self-considered level of the girl in the street?"

There was amazement--even a foreboding--on Shattuck's face as he paused in his walk, and, for the first time speaking anxiously ejaculated, "I swear I don't follow you!"

She went on as if she had not been interrupted, as if she had something to say which had to be said, as if she were reasoning it out for herself: "Take my case. I don't claim that it is uncommon. I do claim that I was not the woman for the situation. I was an only child. My father's marriage had not been happy. I was brought up by a disappointed man on philosophy and pessimism."

"Old sceptics, and modern scoffers. I remember it well."

"Before I was out of my teens, I had imbibed a mistrust for all emotions. Perhaps you did not know that? You may have thought, because they were not all on the outside, that I had none. My poor father had hoped, with his teachings, to save me from future misery. He had probably thought to spare me the commonplace sorrows of love. But he could not."

"There is one thing, my child, that the passing generation cannot do for its heirs--live for them--luckily. Why, you might as well forbid a rose to blossom by word of mouth, as try to thwart nature in a beautiful healthy woman."

"It seems to me that to bring up a woman as I was brought up only prepares her to take the distemper the quicker."

"I do not remember that of you. But I do know that no woman was ever wooed as hotly as you were--or ever--I swear it--more ardently desired. No woman ever led a man the chase you led me. If ever in those days you were as anxious for my love as you have said you were this evening, no one would have guessed it, least of all I."

"My reason had already taught me that mine was but the common fate of all women: that life was demanding of me the usual tribute to posterity: that the sweetness of the emotion was Nature's trick to make it endurable. But according to Nature's eternal plan, my heart could not listen to my head--it beat so loud when you were by, it could not hear, perhaps. But there was something of my father's philosophy left in me, and when I was alone it would speak, and be heard, too. Even when I believed in you--because I wanted to--and half hoped that all my teaching was wrong, I made a bargain with myself. I told myself, quite calmly, that I knew perfectly well all the possibilities of the future. That if I went forward with you, I went forward deliberately with open eyes, knowing what, logically, I might expect to find in the future. Ignorance--that blissful comfort of so many women,--was denied me. Still, the spell of Nature was upon me, and for a time I dreamed that a depth of passionate love like mine, a life of loyal devotion might wrap one man round, and keep him safe--might in fact, work a miracle--and make one polygamous man monogamous. But, even while that hope was in my heart, reason rose up and mocked it, bidding me advance into the Future at my peril. I did it, but I made a bargain with myself, I agreed to abide the consequences--and to abide them calmly."

"And during all those days when I supposed we were so near together--you showed me nothing of this that was in your heart."

"Men and women know very rarely anything of the great struggles that go on in the hearts of one another. Besides, I knew how easily you would reply--naturally. We are all on the defensive in this life. It was with things deeper than words that I was dealing--the things one *does*--not says. Even in the early days of our engagement I knew that I was not as essential to you as you were to me. Life held other interests for you. Even the flattery of other women still had its charm for you. Young as I was, I said to myself: 'If you marry this man--with your eyes open--blame yourself, not him, if you suffer.' I do believe that I have been able to do that."

Shattuck was astride his chair again, his elbows on the back, his chin in his hands. He no longer responded. Words were dangerous. His lips were pressed close together, and there was a long deep line between his eyes.

"My love for you absorbed every other emotion of my life. But I seemed to lack some of the qualities that aid to reconcile other wives to life. I seemed to be without mother-love. My children were dear to me only because they were yours. The maternal passion, which in so many women is the absorbing emotion of life, was denied me. My children were to me merely the tribute to posterity which Life had demanded of me as the penalty of your love--nothing more. I must be singularly unfitted for marriage, because, when the hour came in which I felt that I was no longer your wife, your children seemed no longer mine. They merely represented the next generation--born of me. I know that this is very shocking. I have become used to it,--and, it is the truth. I have not blamed you, I could not--and be reasonable. No man can be other than Nature plans or permits, but how I have pitied myself! I have been through the tempest alone. In spite of reason,--in spite of philosophy--I have suffered from jealousy, from shame, from rage, from self contempt. But that is all past now."

She had not raised her voice, which seemed as without feeling as it was without emphasis. She carefully examined her handkerchief corner by corner, and he noticed for the first time how thin her hands had become.

"Naturally," she went on in that colorless voice, "my first impulse was to be done with life. But I could not bring myself to that, much as I desired it. It would have left you such a wretched memory of me. You could never have pardoned me the scandal--and I felt that I had at least the right to leave you a decent recollection of me."

Shattuck's head fell forward on his arms.--The idea of denial or protest did not occur to him.

The steady voice went monotonously on. "I could not bear to humble you in the eyes of others even by forcing you to face a scandal. I could not bear to humble you in your own eyes by letting you suspect that I knew the truth. I could not bring myself to disturb the outward respectability of your life by interrupting its outward calm. To be absolutely honest--though I had lost you, I could not bring myself to give you up,--as I felt I must, if I let any one discover--most of all you--what I knew. So, like a coward, I lived on, becoming gradually accustomed to the idea that my day was past, but knowing that the moment I was forced to speak, I would be forced to move on out of your life. Singularly enough, as I grew calm, I grew to respect this other woman. I could not blame her for loving you. I ended by admiring her. I had known her so well--she was such a proud woman! I looked back at my marriage and saw the affair as it really was. I had not ***sold*** myself to you exactly--I had loved you too much to bargain in that way; nevertheless, the marriage had been a bargain. In exchange for your promise to protect and provide for me,--to feed me, clothe me, share your fortune with me, and give me your name, I had given you myself,--openly sanctioned by the law, of course--I was too great a coward to have done it otherwise, in spite of the fact that the law gives that same permission to almost any one who asks for it."

"Naomi," he groaned from his covered mouth, "what ghastly philosophy."

"Isn't that the marriage law? How much better am I after all than the poor girl in the street, who is forced to it by misery? To be sure, I believe there is some farcical phrase in the bargain about promising to love none other,--a bare-faced attempt to outwit Nature,--at which Nature laughs. Yet this other woman, proud, high-minded, unselfish, hitherto above reproach, had given herself for love alone--with everything to lose and nothing to gain. I have come to doubt myself. I have had my day. For years it was an enviable one. No woman can hope for more. What right have I to stand in the way of another woman's happiness? A happiness no one can value better than I, who so long wore it in security. I bore my children in peace, with the divine consolation of your devotion about me. What right have I to deny another woman the same joy?"

Shattuck sprang to his feet.

"It's not true!" he gasped. "It's not true!"

The woman never even raised her eyes. She went on carefully inspecting the filmy bit of lace in her hands.

"It ***is*** true," she replied. "Never mind how I discovered it. I know it. That is why she has gone abroad alone. I did not speak until I had to. I am a coward, but not enough of one to bear the thought of her alone in a foreign country with mind and emotions clouded. I may be cowardly enough to wish that I had never found it out,--I am not coward enough to keep silent any longer."

A torrent of words rushed to the man's lips, but he was too wise to make excuses. Yet there were excuses. Any fair-minded judge would have said so. But he knew better than to think that for one moment they would be excuses in the mind of this woman. Besides, the first man's excuse for the first sin has never been viewed with much respect under the modern civilization.

He felt her slowly rise to her feet, and when he raised his head to look at her--not yet fully realizing what had happened to him--all emotion seemed to have become so foreign to her face, that he felt as if she were already a stranger to him.

She took a last look round the room. Her eyes seemed to devour every detail.

"I shall find means to give you your freedom at once."

"You will actually leave me--go away?"

"Can we two remain together now?"

"But your children?"

"Your children, Dick--I have forgotten that I have any. I have had my life. You have still yours to live."

She swept by him down the long room, everything in which was so closely associated with her. Before she reached the door, he was there--and his back against it. She stopped, but she did not look at him. If she could have read the truth in his face, it would have told her that she had never been loved as she was at that moment. All that she had been in her loyalty, her nobility, was so much a part of this man's life. What, compared to that, were petty sins, or big ones? He saw the past as a drowning man sees the panorama of his existence. Yet he knew that everything he could say would be powerless to move her.

It was useless to remind her of their happy years together. They could never be happy again with this between them. It would be equally useless to tell her that this other woman had known, but too well, that he would never desert his wife for her. Had he not betrayed her?

Of what use to tell her how he had repented his folly, that he could never understand it himself? There were the facts, and Nature, and his wife's philosophy against him.

And he had dared be gay the moment the steamer slid into the channel! Was that only this morning? It seemed to be in the last century.

She approached, and stretched her hand toward the door.

He did not move.

"Don't stop me," she pleaded. "Don't make it any harder than it is. Let me take with me the consolation of a decent life together--a decent life decently severed."

He made one last appeal--he opened his arms wide to her.

She shrank back with a shudder, crying out that he should spare her her own contempt--that he should leave her the power to seek peace--and her voice had such a tone of terror, as she recoiled from him, that he felt how powerless any protest would be.

He stepped aside.

Without looking at him she quickly opened the door and passed out.

*   *   *   *   *

The Divorcee nervously rolled up her manuscript.

The usual laugh was not forthcoming. No one dared. Men can't rough-house that kind of a woman.

After a moment's silence the Critic spoke up. "You were right to **read** that story. It is not the sort of thing that lends itself to narrating. Of course you might have acted it out, but you were wise not to."

"I can't help it--got to say it," said the Journalist: "What a horrid woman!"

The Divorcee looked at him in amazement. "How can you say that?" she exclaimed. "I thought I had made her so reasonable. Just what all women ought to be, and what none of us are."

"Thank God for that," said the Journalist. "I'd as lief live in a world created and run by George Bernard Shaw as in one where women were like that."

"Come, come," interrupted the Doctor, who had been eyeing her profile with a curious half amused expression, all through the reading: "Don't let us get on that subject to-night. A story is a story. You have asked, and you have received. None of you seem to really like any story but your own, and I must confess that among us, we are putting forth a strange baggage."

"On the contrary," said the Critic, "I think we are doing pretty well for a crowd of amateurs."

"You are not an amateur," laughed the Journalist, "and yours was the worst yet."

"I deny it," said the Critic. "Mine had real literary quality, and a very dramatic climax."

"Oh, well, if death is dramatic--perhaps. You are the only one up to date who has killed his heroine."

"No story is finished until the heroine is dead," said the Journalist. "This woman,--I'll bet she had another romance."

"Did she?" asked the Critic of the Divorcee, who was still nervously rolling her manuscript in both hands.

"I don't know. How should I? And if I did I shouldn't tell you. It isn't a true story, of course." And she rose from her chair and walked away into the moonlight.

"Do you mean to say," ejaculated the Violinist, who admired her tremendously, "that she made that up in the imagination she carries around under that pretty fluffy hair? I'd rather that it were true--that she had picked it up somewhere."

As we began to prepare to go in, the Doctor looked down the path to where the Divorcee was still standing. After a moment's hesitation he took her lace scarf from the back of her chair, and strolled after her. The Sculptor shrugged his shoulders with such a droll expression that we all had to smile. Then we went indoors.

"Well," said the Doctor, as he joined her--she told me about it afterwards--"was that the way it happened?"

"No, no," replied the Divorcee, petulantly. "That is not a bit the way it happened. That is the way I wish it had happened. Oh, no. I was brought up to believe in the proprietary rights in marriage, and I did what I thought became a womanly woman. I asserted my rights, and made a common or garden row."

The Doctor laughed, as she stamped her foot at him.

"Pardon--pardon," said he. "I was only going to say 'Thank God.' You know I like it best that way."

"I wish I had not told the old story," she said pettishly. "It serves me quite right.

Now I suppose they've got all sorts of queer notions in their heads."

"Nonsense," said the Doctor. "All authors, you know, run the risk of getting mixed up in their romances--think of Charlotte Bronte."

"I'm not an author, and I am going to bed,--to repent of my folly," and she sailed into the house, leaving the Doctor gazing quizzically after her. Before she was out of hearing, he called to her: "I say, you haven't changed a bit since '92."

She heard but she did not answer.

VII

THE LAWYER'S STORY
THE NIGHT BEFORE THE WEDDING
THE TALE OF A BRIDE-ELECT

The next day we all hung about the garden, except the Youngster, who disappeared on his wheel early in the day, and only came back, hot and dusty, at tea-time. He waved a hand at us as he ran through the garden crying: "I'll change, and be with you in a moment," and leapt up the out-side staircase that led to the gallery on which his room opened, and disappeared.

I found an opportunity to go up the other staircase a little later--the Youngster was an old pet of mine, and off and on, I had mothered him. I tapped at the door.

"Can't come in!" he cried.

"Where've you been?"

"Wait there a minute--and mum--. I'll tell you."

So I went and sat in the window looking down the road, until he came, spick and span in white flannels, with his head not yet dried from the douching he had taken.

"See here," he whispered, "I know you can keep a secret. Well, I've been out toward Cambrai--only sixty miles--and I am tuckered. There was a battle there last night--English driven back. They are only two days' march away, and oh! the sight on the roads. Don't let's talk of it."

In spite of myself, I expect I went white, for he exclaimed: "Darn it, I suppose I ought not to have told you. But I had to let off to some one. I don't want to tell the

Doctor. In fact, he forbade my going again."

"Is it a real German victory?" I asked.

"If it isn't I don't know what you'd call it, though such of the English as I saw were in gay enough spirits, and there was not an atmosphere of defeat. Fact is--I kept out of sight and only got stray impressions. Go on down now, or they'll guess something. I'm not going to say a word--yet. Awful sorry now I told you. Force of habit."

I went down. I had hard work for a few minutes to throw the impression off. But the garden was lovely, and tea being over, we all busied ourselves in rifling the flowerbeds to dress the dinner table. If we were going in two days, where was the good of leaving the flowers to die alone? I don't suppose that it was strange that the table conversation was all reminiscent. We talked of the old days: of ourselves when we were boys and girls together: of old Papanti, and our first Cotillion, of Class Days, and, I remembered afterward, that not one of us talked of ourselves except in the days of our youth.

When the coffee came out, we looked about laughing to see which of the three of us left was to tell the story. The Lawyer coughed, tapped himself on his chest, and crossed his long legs.

*   *   *   *   *

It was a cold December afternoon.

The air was piercing.

There had been a slight fall of snow, then a sudden drop in the thermometer preceded nightfall.

Miss Moreland, wrapped in her furs, was standing on a street corner, looking in vain for a cab, and wondering, after all, why she had ventured out.

It was somewhat later than she had supposed, and she was just conventional enough, in spite of her pose to the exact contrary, to hope that none of her friends would pass. She knew her set well enough to know that it would cause something almost like a scandal if she were seen out alone, on foot, on the very eve of her wedding day, when all well bred brides ought to be invisible--repenting their sins, and praying for blessings on the future in theory, but in reality, fussing themselves ill over belated finery.

She had had for some years a number of poor protegees in the lower end of the city, which she had been accustomed to visit on work of a charitable nature begun when she was a school girl. She had found work enough to do there ever since.

It was work of which her father, a hard headed man of business, strongly disapproved, although he was ready enough to give his money. Jack was of her father's mind. She realized that when she returned from the three years' trip round the world, on which she was starting the day after her wedding, she would have other duties, and she knew it would be harder to oppose Jack,--and more dangerous-- than it had been to oppose her father.

In this realization there was a touch of self-reproach. She knew, in her own heart, that she would be glad to do no more work of that sort. Experience had made her hopeless, and she had none of the spiritual support that made women like St. Catherine of Sienna. But, if experience had robbed her of her illusions, she knew, too, that it had set a seal of pain on all the future for her. She could never forget the misery she had seen. So it had been a little in a desire to give one more sop to her conscience, that she had dedicated her last afternoon to freedom to her friends in the very worst part of the town.

If her mother had remained at home, she would never have been allowed to go. All the more reason for returning in good season, and here it was dark! Worse still, the trip had been in every way unsuccessful. She had turned her face home- ward, simply asking herself, as she had done so many times before, if it were "worth while," and answered the question once more with: "Neither to me nor to them." She had already learned, though too young for the lesson, that each individual works out his own salvation,--that neither moral nor physical growth ever works from the surface inward. Opportunity--she could perhaps give that in the future, but she was convinced that those who may give of themselves, and really help in the giving, are elected to the task by something more than the mere desire to serve. In her case the gift of her youth and her illusions had done others no real good, and had more or less saddened her life forever. If she were to really go on with the work, it would only be by giving up the world--her world,--abandoning her life, with its luxury, its love, everything she had been bred to, and longed for. She did not feel a call to do that, so she chose the existence to which she had been born; the love of a man in her own set,--but the shadow of too much knowledge sat on her like a shadow of fear.

She was impatient with herself, the world, living,--and there was no cab in sight.

She looked at her watch. Half past four.

It was foolish not to have driven over, but she had felt it absurd, always, to go about this kind of work in a private carriage, and to-day she could not, as she usually did, take a street car for fear of meeting friends. They thought her queer enough as it was.

An impatient ejaculation escaped her, and like an echo of it she heard a child's voice beside her.

She looked down.

It was a poor miserable specimen. At first she was not quite sure whether it were boy or girl.

Whimpering and mopping its nose with a very dirty hand, the child begged money for a sick mother--a dying mother--and begged as if not accustomed to it-- all the time with an eye for that dread of New England beggars, the man in the blue coat and brass buttons.

Miss Moreland was so consciously irritated with life that she was unusually gentle. She stooped down. The child did not seem six years old. The face was not so very cunning. It was not ugly, either. It was merely the epitome of all that Miss Moreland tried to forget--the little one born without a chance in the world.

With a full appreciation of the child's fear of the police,--begging is a crime in many American towns--she carefully questioned her, watching for the dreaded officer herself.

It was the old story--a dying mother--no father--no one to do anything--a child sent out to cunningly defy the law, but it seemed to be only for bread.

Obviously the thing to do was to deliver the child up to the police. It would be at once properly cared for, and the mother also.

But Miss Moreland knew too much of official charity to be guilty of that.

The easiest thing was to give her money. But, unluckily, she belonged to a society pledged not to give alms in the streets, and her sense of the power of a moral obligation was a strong notion of duty, which had descended to her from her Puritan ancestors. There was one thing left to do.

"Do you know Chardon Street?" she asked.

The child nodded.

There was a flower shop on the corner. She led the child across to it, entered, and asked for an envelope. She wrote a few lines on a card, enclosed it and sealed the envelope. Then she went out to the side-walk again with the child. Stooping over her she made sure that the little one really did know the street. "It isn't far from here," she said. "Give that to any one there, and somebody will go right home with you to see your mother, to warm you, you poor little mite, and feed you, and make you quite happy."

She did not explain, and the child would not have understood, that she vouched for a special donation for the case as a sort of commemorative gift. The sum was large--it was a quixotic sort of salve to a sick conscience which told her that she ought to go herself.

The child, still sobbing, turned away, and drearily started up the hill. She did not go far, however. Miss Moreland had her misgivings on that point. And, just as she was about to draw a breath of relief, convinced that, after all, she would go, the girl stopped deliberately in the shadow of a tree, and sat down on the snow-covered curbstone.

No need to ask what the trouble was. The poor are born with a horror of organized charity. It obliges them to be looked over in all their misery; it presumes a worthiness, or its pretence, which they resent almost as much as they do the intrusion of the visiting committee. This disinclination is as old as poverty, and is the rock ahead of all organized charity. Its exemplification was very trying to Miss Moreland at that moment, and the crouching figure was exasperating.

She pursued the child. She pulled her rather roughly to her feet. It was so provoking to have her sit down in the cold, and to so personify all that she wanted so ardently,--it was purely selfish, she knew that,--to put out of her mind. There seemed but one thing to do: go with the child.

She knew that if she did not, she would not sleep that night, nor smile the next day--and that seemed so unfair to others. Besides, it was not yet so very late.

Bidding the child hurry, she followed her up the hill, and down the other side to a part of the city with which she was not familiar.

The child cried quietly all the way.

Miss Moreland was too vaguely uncomfortable to talk to her, as they hurried along.

It was in front of a dark house that they finally stopped, and went up the stone steps into a hall so dark that she was obliged to take the child's dirty cold hands in hers to be sure of the way.

Perhaps it was a foolish distaste for the contact, combined with her frame of mind, which prevented her from noticing facts far from trifles, which came back to her afterward.

She groped her way up the uncarpeted stairs, and followed her still whimpering guide along what seemed an upper corridor, stumbled on what she immediately knew was the sill of a door, lurched forward as the child let go of her hand, and, before she recovered her balance, the door closed behind her.

She called to the child. No answer.

She felt for the door, found it--it was locked.

She was in perfect darkness.

A terrible wave of sickness passed over her and left her trembling and weak.

All she had ever heard and found it difficult to believe, coursed through her mind.

The folly of it all was worse. Fifteen minutes before all had been well with her--and now--!

Through all her terror one idea was strong within her. She must keep her head, she must be calm, she must be alertly ready for whatever happened.

The whole thing had seemed so simple. The crying child had been so plausible! Yet--to enter a strange dark house, in an unknown part of the city! How absurd it was of her! And that--after noticing--as she had--that, cold as the halls were and uncarpeted, there was neither smell of dirt nor humanity in the air!

While all these thoughts pursued one another through her mind she stood erect just inside the door.

She really dared not move.

Suddenly a fear came to her that she might not be alone. For a moment that fear dominated all other sensations. She held her breath, in a wild attempt to hear she knew not what.

It was deathly still!

She backed to the door, and began cautiously feeling her way along the wall. Inch by inch, she crept round the room, startled almost to fainting at each obstacle she encountered.

It was a large room with an alcove--a bedroom. There was but little furniture, one door only, two windows covered with heavy drapery, the windows bolted down, and evidently shuttered on the outside.

When she returned to the door, one thing was certain, she was alone. The only danger she need apprehend must come through that one door.

Yet she pushed a chair against the wall before she sat down to wait--for what? Ah, that was the horror of it! Was it robbery? There was her engagement ring, a few ornaments like her watch, and very little money! Yet, as she had seen misery, even that might be worth while. But was this a burglar's method? A ransom? That was too mediaeval for an American city. If neither, then what?

She had but one enemy in the world, her Jack's best friend, or at least, he was his best friend until the days of her engagement. But he was a gentleman, and these were the days when men did not revenge themselves on women who frankly rejected the attentions they had never encouraged. It was weak, she knew it, to even remember the words he had said to her when she had refused to hear the man she was to marry slandered by his chum--still she wished now that she had told Jack, all the same.

If she could only have a light! There was gas, but no matches. To sit in the dark, waiting, she knew not what, was maddening.

Then a new terror came over her. Suppose she should fall asleep from fatigue and exhaustion, and the effect of the dark?

It seemed days that she sat there.

She knew afterward that it was only five hours and a half, but that five hours and a half were an eternity--three hundred and thirty minutes, each one of which dragged her down, like a weight, into the black abyss of the unknown; three hundred and thirty minutes of listening to the labored beating of her own heart--it was an age, after all!

Only once did she lose control of herself. She imagined she heard voices in the hall--that some one laughed--was there still laughter in the world? In spite of herself, she rushed to the door, and pounded on it. This was so useless that she began to cry hysterically. Yet she knew how foolish that was, and she stumbled back to her chair, sank into it, and calmed herself. She would not do that again.

What was her mother thinking? Poor mama! What would Jack say, when, at eleven o'clock, he ran in from his bachelor's dinner--his last--which he was giving to a few friends? What would her father say? He had always prophesied some disaster for her excursions into the slums.

Her imagination could easily picture the mad search that would be made--but who could find a trace of her?

The blackness, the fear, the dread, were doing their work! She was numb! She began to feel as if she were suspended in space, as if everything had dropped away from her, as if in another instant she would fall--and fall--and fall--.

Suddenly she heard a laugh in the hall again--this time there was no mistake about it, for it was followed by several voices. Some one approached the door.

A key was inserted and turned in the lock.

She started to her feet, and steadied herself!

The door swung open quickly--some one entered. By the dim light in the hall behind, she saw that it was a man--a gentleman in evening clothes, with a hat on the back of his head, and a coat over his arm.

But while her alert senses took that in, the door closed again--the man had remained inside.

The thought of making a dash for the door came to her, but it was too late.

She heard the scratching of a match--a muttered oath at the darkness in a thick voice--then a sudden flood of light blinded her.

She drew her hands quickly across her eyes, and was conscious that the man had flung his hat and coat on the bed before he turned to face her.

In a moment all her fear was gone.

She stumbled weakly as she ran toward him, crying hysterically, "Jack, dear Jack, how did you find me? I should have gone mad if you had been much later! Take me home! Take me home--"

Had Miss Moreland fainted, as a well-conducted girl of her class ought to have done, this would have been a very different kind of a story.

Unluckily, or luckily, according as one views life--in the relief of his presence, all danger of that fled. Unluckily for him, also, the appearance of his bride-elect in such an unexpected place was so appalling to him that his nerve failed him entirely. Instead of clasping her in his arms as he should have done, he had the decency to recoil, and cover his face instinctively from her eyes.

Miss Moreland stopped as if turned to stone.

She was conscious at first of but one thing--he had not expected to find her there. He had not come to seek her. Then, for what?

A sudden flash illumined her ignorance, and behind it she grasped at the vague accusation her other suitor had tried to make to her unwilling ears.

Her outstretched hands fell to her sides.

He still leaned against the wall, where the shock had flung him. The exciting fumes of the wine he had drunk too recklessly evaporated, and only a dim recollection remained in his absolutely sobered brain of the idiotic wager, the ugly jest, the still more contemptible bravado that had sent him into this hell.

He did not attempt to speak.

When her strained voice said: "Take me home, please," he started and the fear that had been on her face was now on his. A hundred dangers, of which she did not dream, stood between that room and a safe exit in which she should not be seen, and that much of this wretched business--which he understood now only too well--miscarry.

He started for the door. "Stay here," he said. "You are perfectly safe," and he went out, and closed and locked the door behind him.

For the man who plotted without, and the woman who sat like a stone within that room, the next half hour were equally horrible. But time was no longer measured by her!

She never remembered much more of that evening. She had a vague recollection that he came back. She had a remembrance that he had helped her stand--given her a glass of water--and led her down the uncarpeted stairs out into the street. Then she was conscious that she walked a little way. Then that she had been helped into a carriage, and then she had jolted and jolted and jolted over the pavings, always with his pale face opposite, and she knew that his eyes were full of pity. Then everything seemed to stop, but it was only the carriage that had come to a standstill. She was in front of her own door.

A voice said in her ear, "Can you stand?" And she knew she was on the steps. She heard the bell ring, but before her mother could catch her in her arms as she fell, she heard the carriage door bang, and he was gone forever.

All that night she lay and tossed and wept and raved, and longed in her fever to die.

And all night, he walked the streets marvelling at himself, at Nature, and at Civilization, between which he had so disastrously fallen, and wondering to how many men the irremediable had ever happened before.

And the next morning, early, messengers were flying about with notices of the bride's illness.--Miss Moreland's wedding was deferred by brain fever.

When she recovered, her hair was white, and she had lost all taste for matrimony, but she had found instead that desire for anything rather than personal existence, which made her the ardent, self-abnegating worker for the welfare of the downtrodden that the world knew her.

*   *   *   *   *

There was a moment of surprised silence.

Some one coughed. No one laughed. Then the Journalist, always ready to leap into a breach, gasped: "Horrible!"

"Getting to be a pet word of yours," said the Lawyer.

The Violinist tried to save the situation by saying gently: "Well, I don't know. It is the commonest of all situations in a melodrama. So why fuss?"

The Trained Nurse shrugged her shoulders. "I know that story," she said.

"You do not," snapped the Lawyer. "You may know *a* story, but you never heard that one."

"All right," she admitted. "I am not going to add footnotes, don't be alarmed."

"You don't mean to say that is a true story?" ejaculated the Divorcee.

"As for me," said the Critic, "I don't believe it."

"No one asked you to," replied the Lawyer. "It is only another case of the Doctor's pet theory--that whatever the mind of mortal mind can conceive, can come to pass."

"I suppose also that it is a proof of another of his pet theories. Scratch civilized man, and you find the beast."

The Doctor was lying back in his chair. He never said a word. Somehow the story seemed a less suggestive topic of conversation than usual.

"The weather is going to change," said the Doctor. "There's rain in the air."

"Well, anyway," said the Journalist, as we gathered up our belongings and prepared to shut up for the night, "the Youngster's ghost story was a good night cap compared to that."

"Not a bit of it," said the Critic. "There's the foundation of a bully melodrama in that story, and I'm not sure that it isn't the best one yet--so full of reserves."

"No imagination, all the same," answered the Critic. "As realistic in subject, if not in treatment, as Zola."

"Now give us some shop jargon," laughed the Lawyer. "You've not really treated us to a true touch of your methods yet."

"I only do that," laughed the Critic, "when I'm getting paid for it. After all, as the Violinist remarked, the situation is a favorite one in melodrama, from the money-coining 'Two Orphans' down. The only trouble is, the Lawyer poured his villain and hero into one mould. The other man ought to have trapped her, and the hero rescued her. But that is only the difference between reality and art. Life is inartistic. Art is only choosing the best way. Life never does that."

"Pig's wrist," said the Doctor, and that settled the question.

VIII

THE JOURNALIST'S STORY
IN A RAILWAY STATION
THE TALE OF A DANCER

On Friday night, just as we were finishing dinner--we had eaten inside--the Divorcee said: "It may not be in order to make the remark, but I cannot help saying that it is so strange to think that we are sitting here so quietly in a country at war, suffering for nothing, very little inconvenienced, even by the departure of all the men. The field work seems to be going on just the same. Every one seems calm. It is all most unexpected and strange to me."

"I don't see it that way at all," said the Journalist. "I feel as if I were sitting on a volcano, knowing it was going to erupt, but not knowing at what moment."

"That I understand," said the Divorcee, "but that is not exactly what I mean. I meant that, in spite of *that* feeling which every one between here and Paris must have, I see no outward signs of it."

"They are all about us just the same," remarked the Doctor, "whether you see them or not. Did it ever happen to you to be walking in some quiet city street, near midnight, when all the houses were closed, and only here and there a street lamp gleamed, and here and there a ray of light filtered through the shuttered window of some silent house, and to suddenly remember that inside all these dark walls the tragedies of life were going on, and that, if a sudden wave of a magician's wand were to wipe away the walls, how horrified, or how amused one would be?"

"Well," said the Lawyer, "I have had that idea many times, but it has come to me more often in some hotel in the mountains of Switzerland. I remember one night sitting on the terrace at Murren, with the Jungfrau rising in bridal whiteness above the black sides of the Schwarze-Monch, and the moon shining so brightly over the slopes, that I could count any number of isolated little chalets perched on the ledges, and I never had the feeling so strongly of life going on with all its joys and griefs and crimes, invisible, but oppressive."

"I am afraid," said the Doctor, "that there is enough of it going on right here--if we only knew it. I had an example this afternoon. I was walking through the village, when an old woman called to me, and asked if I were the doctor from the old Grange. I said I was, and she begged me to come in and see her daughter-in-law. She was very ill, and the local doctor is gone. I found a young, very pretty girl, with a tiny baby, in as bad a state of hysteria as I ever saw. But that is not the story. That I heard by degrees. It seems the father-in-law, a veteran of 1870, now old, and nearly helpless, is of good family, but married, in his middle age, a woman of the country. They had one son who was sent away to school, and became a civil engineer. He married, about two years ago, this pretty girl whom I saw. She is Spanish. He met her somewhere in Southern Spain, and it was a desperate love match. The first child was born about six weeks before the war broke out. Of course the young husband was in the first class mobilized. The young wife is not French. She doesn't care at all who governs France, so that her man were left her in peace. I imagine that the old father suspected this. He had never been happy that his one son married a foreigner. The instant the young wife realized that her man was expected to put love of France before love of her, she began to make every effort to induce him to go out of the country. To make a long story short, the son went to his mother, whom he adored, made a clean breast of the situation, and proposed that, to satisfy his wife, he should start with her for the Spanish frontier, finding means to have her brother meet them there and take her home to her own people. He promised to make no effort to cross the frontier himself, and gave his word of honor to be with his regiment in time. He knew it would not be easy to do, and, in case of accident, he wished his mother to be able to explain to the old veteran. But the lad had counted without the spirit that is dominant in every French woman to-day. The mother listened. She controlled herself. She did not protest. But that night, when the young couple were about to leave the house, carrying the sleeping baby, they found the old man, pistol in hand, with his back against the door. The words were few. The veteran stated that his son could only pass over his dead body--that if he insisted, he would shoot him before he would allow him to pass: that neither wife nor child should leave France. It was in vain that the wife, on her knees, pleaded that she was not French--that the war did not concern her--that her husband was dearer to her than honor--and so forth. The old man declared that in marrying his son she became French, though she was a disgrace to the name, that her son was a born Frenchman; that she might go, and welcome, but that she would go without the child, and, of course, that ended the argument. The next morning the baby was christened, but the tale had leaked out. I suppose the Spanish wife had not kept her ideas absolutely to herself--and the son joined his regiment. The Spanish wife is still here, but, needless to say, she is not at all loved by her husband's family, who watch her like lynxes for fear she will abduct the child, and she has developed as neat a case of hysterical mania of persecution as I ever encountered. So you see that even in this quiet place there are tragedies behind the walls. But I seem to be telling a story out of my turn!"

"And a forbidden war story, at that," said the Youngster. "So to change the air--whose turn is it?"

The Journalist puffed out his chest. "Ladies and gentlemen," he said, as he rose to his feet, and struck, the traditional attitude of a monologist, "I regret to inform you that you will be obliged to have a taste of my histrionic powers. I've got to act out part of this story--couldn't seem to tell it in any other form."

$$* \qquad * \qquad * \qquad * \qquad *$$

"Dora!"

A slender young woman turned at the word, so sharply spoken over her shoulder, and visibly paled.

She was strikingly attractive, in her modish tailor frock, and her short tight jacket of Persian lamb, with its high, collar of grey fur turned up to her ears.

Her singularly fair skin, her red hair, her brown eyes, with dark lashes, and narrowly pencilled eyebrows that were almost black, gave her a remarkable look, and at first sight suggested that Nature had not done it all. But a closer observation convinced one that the strange combination of such hair and such eyebrows was only one of those freaks by which Nature now and then warns the knowing to beware even of marvellous beauty. In this case it stamped a woman as one who--by several signs--might be identified by the initiated as one of those, who, without reason or logic, spring now and again from most unpromising soil!

She had walked the entire length of the station from the wide doors on the street side to the swing doors at the opposite end which gave entrance to the tracks.

As she passed, no man had failed to turn and look after her, as, with her well hung skirts just clearing the wet pavement, she stepped daintily over the flagging, and so lightly that neither boots nor skirt were the worse for it. One sees women in Paris who know that art, but it is rare in an American.

She must have been long accustomed to attracting masculine eyes, and no wonder, for when she stepped into the place she seemed to give a color to the atmosphere, and everything and everybody went grey and commonplace beside her.

It was a terrible night in November.

The snow was falling rapidly outside, and the wind blew as it can blow only on the New England coast.

It was the sort of night that makes one forced to be out look forward lovingly to home, and think pityingly of the unfortunate, while those within doors involuntarily thank God for comfort, and hug at whatever remnant of happiness living has left them.

The railway station was crowded.

The storm had come up suddenly at the close of a fair day. It was the hour, too, at which tradespeople, clerks, and laborers were returning home to the suburbs, and at which the steamboat express for New York was being made up--although it was not an encouraging night for the latter trip.

The pretty young woman with the red hair had looked through the door near the tracks, and glanced to the right, where the New York express should be. The gate was still closed. She was much too early! For a second she hesitated. She glanced about quickly, and the look was not without apprehension. It was evident that she did not see the man who was following her, and who seemed to have been waiting for her near the outer door. He did not speak, nor attract her attention in any way.

The crowd served him in that!

After a moment's hesitation, she turned toward the ladies' waiting room, and just as she was about to enter, the man behind addressed her--and the word was said so low that no one near heard it--though, by the start she gave, it might have been a pistol shot.

"Dora!"

She stood perfectly still. The color died out of her face; but only for an instant. She looked alarmed, then perplexed, and then she smiled. She was evidently a young woman of resources.

The man was a stalwart handsome fellow of his class--though it was almost impossible to guess what that was save that it was not that which the world labels by exterior signs "gentleman." He might easily have been some sort of a mechanic. He was certainly neither a clerk nor the follower of any of the unskilled professions. He was surely countrybred, for there was a largeness in his expression as well as his bearing that spoke distinctly of broad vistas and exercise. He was tall and broad-shouldered. He stood well on his feet, hampered as little by his six feet of height and fourteen stone weight as he was by the size of his hands. One would have easily backed him to ride well and shoot straight, though he probably never saw the inside of what is called a "drawing-room."

There was the fire of a mighty emotion in his deep-set eyes. There were signs of a tremendous animal force in his square chin and thick neck, but it was balanced well by his broad brow and wide-set eyes. He seemed at this moment to hold himself in check with a rigid stubbornness that answered for his New England origin, and Puritan ancestry! Indeed, at the moment he addressed the woman, but for his eyes, he might have seemed as indifferent as any of the stone figures that upheld the iron girders of the roof above him!

Still smiling archly she moved forward into the waiting room and, passing through the dense crowd that hung about the door, crossed the room to an open space.

Without a word the man followed.

The room was dimly lighted. The crowd that surged about them, coming and going, and sometimes pressing close on every side, seemed not to note them. And, if they had, they would have seen nothing more remarkable than an extremely pretty young woman conversing quietly with a big fellow in a reefer and long boots--a rig he carried well.

"Dora!" he said again, and then had to pause to steady his voice.

Dora wet her red lips with the pointed tip of her tiny tongue; swallowed nervously once or twice, before she spoke. She was now facing him, and still smiling.

He kept his eyes fixed on her face. He did not respond to the smile. His eyes were tragic. He seemed to be seeking something in her face as if he feared her mere words would not help him.

"Why, Zeke," she said at last, when she realized that he could not get beyond her name, "I thought you had gone home an hour ago! Why didn't you take the 5.15 train?"

"I changed my mind! To tell you the truth, I heard that you were in town this afternoon. I have been watching for you--for some time."

"Well, all I can say is--you are foolish. Where's the good for you fretting yourself so? I can take care of myself."

"I can't get used to you being about in the city streets alone."

"How absurd!"

"I have been absurd a great many times of late--in your eyes. Our ideas don't seem to agree any more."

"No, Zeke, they don't!"

"Why speak to me in that tone, Dora? Don't do it!"

He looked over her head, as if to be sure of his hold on himself. He was ghastly white about his smooth-shaven, thick lips. Both hands were thrust deep into his reefer pockets.

"What's come to you, Zeke?" she asked nervously. His was not exactly the face one would see unmoved!

He answered her without looking at her. It was evident he did not dare just yet. "Nothing much, I reckon. I've been a bit down all day. I really don't know why, myself. I've had a queer presentiment, as if something were going to happen. As if something terrible were coming to me."

"Well, I'm sorry. You've no occasion to feel like that, I'm sure."

"All right, if you say so. What train shall we take?"

He stretched out one hand to take the small bag she carried.

She shrank back instinctively, and withdrew the bag. He must have felt rather than seen the movement, it was so slight.

His hand fell to his side.

Still, he persisted.

"I'm dead done up, Dora. I need my dinner, come on!"

"Then you'd better take the 6.00 train. You've just time," she said hurriedly.

"All right. Come on!"

He laid his hand on her shoulder with a gesture that was entreating. It was the first time he had touched her. A frightened look came into her eyes. He did not see it, for he was still avoiding her face. It was as if he were afraid of reading something there he did not wish to know.

Her red lips had taken on a petulant expression--that of one who hated to be "stirred up." In a childish voice--which only thinly veiled an obstinate determination--she pouted: "I'm not going--yet."

The words were said almost under her breath, as if she were fearful of their effect on him, yet was determined to carry her point.

But the man only sighed deeply as he replied: "I thought your dancing lessons were over. I hoped I was no longer to spend my evenings alone. Alone! Looking round at the things that are yours, and among which I feel so out of place, except when you are there to make me forget. God! What damnable evenings I've spent there--feeling as if you were slipping further and further out of my life--as if you were gone, and I had only the clothes you had worn, an odor about me somewhere to convince me that I had not dreamed you! Sometimes that faint, indistinct, evasive scent of you in the room has almost driven me out of my head. I wonder I haven't killed you before now--to be sure of you! I'm afraid of Hell, I suppose, or I should have."

The woman did not look at all alarmed. Indeed there was a light in her amber eyes that spoke of a kind of gratification in stirring this young giant like that--this huge fellow that could so easily crush her--but did not! She knew better why than he did--but she said nothing.

With his eyes still fixed on space--after a pause--he went on: "I was fool enough to believe that that was all over, at last, that you had danced to your heart's content, and that we were to begin the old life--the life before that nonsense--over again.

You were like my old Dora all day yesterday! The Dora I loved and courted and married back there in the woods. But I might have known it wasn't finished by the ache I had here," and he struck himself a blow over the heart with his clenched fist, "when I waked this morning, and by the weight I've carried here all day." And he drew a deep breath like one in pain.

The woman looked about as if apprehensive that even his passionate undertone might have attracted attention, but only a man by the radiator seemed to have noticed, and he had the air of being not quite sober enough to understand.

There was a long pause.

The woman glanced nervously at the clock.

The man was again staring over her head.

It was quarter to six. Her precious minutes were flying. She must be rid of him!

"See here, Zeke, dear," she said, in desperation, speaking very rapidly under her breath--no fear but he would hear--"the truth is, that I'm not a bit better satisfied with our sordid kind of life than I was a year ago, when we first discussed it. I'm awfully sorry! You know that. But I can't change--and there is the whole truth! It's not your fault in one way--and yet in one way it is. God knows you have done everything you could, and more some ways than you ought. But, unluckily for you, gratifying me was not the way to mend the situation for yourself. It is cruel--but it is the truth! If a man wants to keep a woman of my disposition attached to him, he'd do far better to beat her than over-educate her, and teach her all the beauties of freedom. He should keep her ignorant, rather than cultivate her imagination, and open up the wonders of the world to her. It's rough on chaps like you, that with all your cleverness you've no instinct to set you right on a point like this--but it is lucky for women like me--at times! You were determined to force all this out of me, so you may as well hear the whole brutal truth. I'm sick of our stupid ways of life--I have been sick of it for a long time. I've passed all power to pretend any longer. I have learned that there is a great and beautiful world within the reach of women who are clever enough and brave enough to grasp at an opportunity, without looking forward or back. I want to walk boldly to this. I'm not afraid of the stepping-stones! This is really all your fault. When you married me, five years ago, I was only sixteen, and very much in love with you. Now, why didn't you make me do the housework and drudge as all the other women on the farms about yours did? I'd have done it then, and willingly, even to the washing and scrubbing. I had been working in a cotton mill. I didn't know anything better than to drudge. I thought that was a woman's lot. It didn't even seem terrible to me. But no--you set yourself to amuse me. You brought me way up to town on a wedding journey. For the first time in my life I saw there idle women in the world, who wore soft clothes and were always dressed up. You bought me finery. I was clever and imitative. I pined for all the excitement and beauty of city life when we were back on the farm, in the life you loved. I cried for it, as a child cries for the moon. I never dreamed of getting it. And you surprised me by selling the farm, and coming nearer the town to live. Just because I had an ear for music, and could pick out tunes on the old melodeon, I must have a piano and take lessons. Just because my music teacher happened to be French and I showed an aptitude for studying, that must be gratified. Can you really blame me if I want to see more of the wide world that opened up to me? Did you really think French novels and music were likely to make a woman of my lively imagination content with her lot as wife of a mechanic--however clever?"

The man looked down at her as if stunned. Arguments of that sort were a bit above the reasoning of the simple masculine animal, who seemed to belong to that race which comprehends little of the complex emotions, and looks on love as the one inevitable passion of life, and on marriage as its logical result and everlasting conclusion.

It was probable at this moment that he completed his alphabet in the great lesson of life--and spelled out painfully the awful truth, that not all the royal service of worship and love in a man's heart can hold a woman.

There was something akin to a sob in his throat as he replied: "You were so young--so pretty! I could not bear to think that you should soil your hands for me! I wanted to make up to you for all the hardships and sorrows of your childhood. I dreamed of being mother and father as well as husband to you. I thought it would make you happy to owe everything to me--as happy as it made me to give. I would willingly have carried you every step of your life, rather than you should have tired your feet. Is that a sin in a woman's eyes?"

A whimsical smile broke over the woman's face. It quivered on her red lips for just a breath, as if conscious how ill-timed it was. "I really like to tire my feet," she murmured, and she pointed the toe of her tiny boot, as if poised to dance, and looked down on it with evident admiration.

The man caught his breath sharply.

"It's that damned dancing that has upset you, Dora!"

"Sh! Don't swear! I do like dancing! I have always told you so. It was you who first admired it. It was you who let me learn."

"You were my wife! I thought that meant everything to you that it meant to me. I loved your beauty because it was yours; your pleasures because they gave you pleasure. All my ideas of right and wrong in marriage which I learned in my father's honest house bent to your desires and happiness."

She looked nervously at the clock. Ten minutes to six.

"Dora--for God's sake look at me! Dora--you're not leaving me?"

It was an almost inarticulate cry, as of a man who had foreseen his doom, and only protested from some unconquerable instinct to struggle!

She patted his clenched hand gently.

It was plainly evident that she hated the sight of suffering, and hated more not having her own way, and was possessed by a refined kind of cowardice.

"Don't make a row, there's a dear boy! It is like this: I am going over to New York, just for a few weeks. I would have told you yesterday, only I hated spoiling a nice day. It was a nice day?--with a scene. You'll find a nice long letter at home--it's a sweet one, too--telling you all about it. Don't take it too hard! I am going to earn fifty dollars a week--just fancy that--and don't blame me too much!"

He didn't seem to hear! He hung his head--the veins in his forehead swelled--there were actually tears in his eyes--and the mighty effort he made to restrain a sob was terrible--and six feet of American manhood, as fine a specimen of the animal as the soil can show, animated by a spirit which represented well the dignity of toil and self-respect, stood bowed down with ungovernable grief and shame before a merely ornamental bit of femininity.

Fate had simply perpetrated another of her ghastly pleasantries!

The woman was perplexed--naturally! But it was evidently the sight of her work, and not the work, itself, that pained her.

"Don't cut up so rough, Zeke, please don't," she went on. "I'm very fond of you--you know that--but I detest the odor of the shop, and it is so easy for us both to escape it."

He shrank as if she had struck him.

Instinctively he must have remembered the cotton mill from which he took her. A man rarely understands a woman's faculty for forgetting--that is to say, no man of his class does.

"Doesn't it seem a bit selfish of you," she went on, "to object to my earning nearly three times what you can--and so easily--and prettily?"

"I wanted you to be happy with what I could give you."

"Well, I'm sorry, but I'm not. No use to fib about it! It is too late. Your notions are so queer."

"I suppose it is queer to love one woman--and to love her so that laboring for her is happiness! I suppose you do find me a queer chap, because I am not willing that my wife--flesh of my flesh--should flaunt herself, half dressed, to excite the admiration of other men--all for fifty dollars a week!"

"See here, Zeke, you are making too much of this! If it is the separation you can't stand--why come, too! I'll soon enough be getting my hundred a week, and more. That is enough for both of us. You can be with me, if that is what you mind!"

"If that is what I mind? You know better than that! Am I such a cur that you think, if there were no other reason, I'd pose before the world as the husband of a woman who owes nothing to him--as if I were--"

She interrupted him sharply.

"What odds does it make--tell me that--which of us earns the money? To have it is the only important thing!"

The man straightened up--and squared his broad shoulders. A strange change came over him.

He laid his heavy hand on her shoulder, and, for the first time, he spoke with a disregard for self-control, although he did not raise his voice.

"Look at me, Dora, and be sure I mean what I say. Leave me to-day, and don't you ever come back to me. It may kill me to live without you. Well, better that than--than the other! I married you to live with you--not merely to have you! I've been a faithful husband to you! I shall remain that while I live. I never denied you anything I could get for you! But this I will not put up with! I thought you loved me--even if you were sometimes vain, and now and then cruel. If you're ill--if you disappoint yourself, I'll be ready to take care of you--as I promised. But don't never dare to come back to me otherwise! Unless you're in want and homeless, unless you can't live, but by the labor of my hands, I'll never sleep under the same roof with you again. Never!"

"What nonsense, Zeke! Of course I'll come back! You won't turn me away! I only want to see a little of the world, to get a few of the things you can't give me-- no blame to you, either!"

He did not seem to hear her.

Almost as if speaking to himself, he went on: "I've feared for some time you didn't love me. I didn't want to believe it. I was a coward. I shut my eyes. I took what you gave me--I daren't think of this--which has come to me! I dared not! God punishes idolatry! He has punished mine. Be sure you're not making a mistake, Dora! There may be other men will admire you, my girl--will any of them love you as I do? There's never a minute I'm not conscious of you, sleeping or waking. Think again, Dora, before you leave me!"

"I can't, Zeke. I've signed a contract. I couldn't reconsider if I wanted to. It's just seven minutes to train time. Kiss me--there's a dear lad--and don't row me any more!"

She raised herself on tip toes and approached her red lips to his face--lips of an intense color to go with the marked pallor of the rest of the face, and which surely were never offered to him in vain before--but he was beyond their seduction at last.

"You've decided?" he said.

"Of course!"

"All right! Good-bye, then! You promised to cleave to me through thick and thin 'till death did us part.' I'll have no halfway business," and he turned on his heel, and without looking back he pushed his way through the crowd, which chatted and fussed and never even noted the passing of a broken heart.

The pretty creature watched him out of sight.

There was a humorous pout on her lips. But she seemed so sure of her man! He would come back, of course--when she called him--if she ever did! Probably she liked him better at that moment than she had liked him in two years. He had op- posed her. He had defied her power over him. He had once more become a man to conquer--if she ever had time!

But just now there was something more important. That train! It was three minutes to the schedule time.

As he disappeared into the crowd she drew a breath of relief, and hurried out of the waiting room and pushed her way to the platform, along which she hurried to the parlor car, where she seated herself comfortably, as if no man with a broken life had been set down that day against her record.

To be sure, she could not quite rid herself of thoughts of his face, but the recollection rather flattered her, and did not in the least prevent her noticing the looks of admiration with which two men on the opposite side of the car were regarding her.

Once or twice she glanced out of the window, apparently alternately expecting and dreading to see her stalwart husband come sprinting down the platform for the kiss he had refused.

He didn't come!

She was relieved as the train started--yet she hated to feel he could really let her go like that!

She never guessed at the depth of suffering she had brought him. How could she appreciate what she could never feel? She never dreamed that as the train pulled out into the storm he stood at the end of the station, and watched it slowly round the curve under the bridge and pass out of sight. No one was near to see him turn aside, and rest his arms against the brick wall, to bury his face in them, and sob like a child, utterly oblivious of the storm that beat upon him.

*   *   *   *   *

And he sat down.

"Come on," yelled the Youngster, "where's the claque?" And he began to applaud furiously.

"Oh, if there is a claque, the rest of us don't need to exert ourselves," said the Lawyer, indolently.

"But I say," asked the Youngster, after the Journalist had made his best bow. "I

AM disappointed. Was that all?"

"My goodness," commented the Doctor, as he lighted a fresh cigar. "Isn't that enough?"

"Not for *me*," replied the Youngster. "I want to know about her *debut*. Was she a success?"

"Of course," answered the Journalist. "That sort always is."

"And I want to know," insisted the Youngster, "what became of him?"

"Why," ejaculated the Sculptor, "of course he cut his big brown throat!"

"Not a bit of it," said the Critic. "He probably went up to New York, and hung round the stage door."

"Until she called in the police, and had him arrested as a common nuisance," added the Lawyer.

"I'll bet my microscope he didn't," laughed the Doctor.

"And you won't lose your lens," replied the Journalist. "He never did a blooming thing--that is, he didn't if he existed."

"Oh, my eyes," said the Youngster. "I am disappointed again. I thought that was a simon-pure newspaper yarn--one of your reporter's dodges--real journalese!"

"She is true enough," answered the Journalist, "and her feet are true, and so is her red hair, and, unless she is a liar, and most actresses are, so is he and her origin, but as for the way she cut him out--well, I had to make that up. It is better than any of the six tales she told as many interviewers, in strict secrecy, in the days when she was collecting hearts and jewels and midnight suppers in New York."

"Is she still there?" asked the Youngster, "because if she is, I'll go back and take a look at Dora myself--after the war!"

"Well, Youngster," laughed the Journalist, "it will have to be 'after the war,' as you will probably have to go to Berlin to find her."

"That's all right!" retorted the Youngster. "I *am* going--with the Allied armies."

We all jumped up.

"No!" cried the Divorcee. "No!!"

"But I am. Where's the good of keeping it secret? I enlisted the day I went to Paris the first time--so did the Doctor, so did the Critic, and so did *he*, the innocent looking old blackguard," and he seized the Journalist by both shoulders and shook him well. "He thought we wouldn't find it out."

"Oh, well," said the Journalist, "when one has seen three wars, one may as well see one more.--This will surely be my last."

"Anyway," cried the Youngster, "we'll see it all round--the Doctor in the Field Ambulance, me in the air, the Critic is going to lug litters, and as for the Journalist--well, I'll bet it's secret service for him! Oh, I know you are not going to tell, but I saw you coming out of the English Embassy, and I'll bet my machine you've a ticket for London, and a letter to the Chief in your pocket."

"Bet away," said the Critic.

"What'd I tell you--what'd I tell you? He speaks every God-blessed language going, and if it wasn't that, he'd tell fast enough."

"Never mind," said the Trained Nurse, "so that he goes somewhere--with the rest of us."

"You--YOU?" exclaimed the Divorcee.

"Why not? I was trained for this sort of thing. This is my chance."

"And the rest of us?"

The Doctor intervened. "See here, this is forty-eight hours or more earlier than I meant this matter to come up. I might have known the Youngster could not hold his tongue."

"I've been bursting for three days."

"Well, you've burst now, and I hope you are content. There is nothing to worry about, yet. We fellows are leaving September 1st. The roads are all clear, and it was my idea that we should all start for Paris together early next Tuesday morning. I don't know what the rest of you want to do, but I advise *you*," turning to the Divorcee, "to go back to the States. You would not be a bit of good here. You may be there."

"You are quite right," she replied sadly. "I'd be worse than no good. I'd need 'first aid,' at the first shot."

"I'm going with her," said the Sculptor. "I'd be more useless than she would." And he turned a questioning look at the Lawyer.

"I must go back. I've business to attend to. Anyway, I'd be an encumbrance here. I may be useful there. Who knows?"

As for me, every one knew what I proposed to do, and that left every one accounted for except the Violinist. He had been in his favorite attitude by the tree, just as he had been on that evening when it had been proposed to "tell stories," gazing first at one and then at another, as the hurried conversation went on.

"Well," he said, finding all eyes turned on him, "I am going to London with the Journalist--if he is really going."

"All right, I am," was the reply.

"And from London I shall get to St. Petersburg. I have a dream that out of all this something may happen to Poland. If it does, I propose to be there. I'll be no good at holding a gun--I could never fire one. But if, by some miracle, there comes out of this any chance for the 'Fair Land of Poland' to crawl out, or be dragged out, from under the feet of the invader--well, I'll go *home*--and--and--"

He hesitated.

"And grow up with the country," shouted the Youngster. "Bully for you."

"I may only go back to fiddle over the ruins. But who knows? At all events, I'll go back and carry with me all that your country had done for three generations of my family. They'll need it."

"Well," said the Doctor, "that is all settled. Enough for to-night. We'll still have one or two, and it may be three days left together. Let us make the most of them. They will never come again."

"And to think what a lovely summer we had planned," sighed the Divorcee.

"Tush!" ejaculated the Doctor. "We had a lovely time all last year. As for this summer, I imagine that it has been far finer than what we planned. Anyway, let us be thankful that it was *this* summer that we all found one another again."

"Better go to bed," cried the Critic; "the Doctor is getting sentimental--a bad sign in an army surgeon."

"I don't know," remarked the Trained Nurse; "I've seen those that were more sentimental than the Journalist, and none the worse for it."

IX

THE VIOLINIST'S STORY
THE SOUL OF THE SONG
THE TALE OF A FIANCEE

On Saturday most of the men made a run into Paris.

It had finally been decided as best that, if all went well, we should leave for Paris some time the next day. There were steamer tickets to attend to. There were certain valuables to be taken up to the Bank. The Divorcee had a trunk or two that she thought she ought to send in order that we might start with as little luggage as possible, so both chauffeurs were sent up to town with baggage, and orders to wait there. The rest of us had been busy doing a little in the way of dismantling the house. The unexpected end of our summer had come. It was sad, but I imagine none of us were sorry, under the circumstances, to move on.

It was nearly dinner time when the cars came back, almost together, and we were surprised to see the Doctor going out to the servants' quarters instead of joining us as he usually did. In fact, we did not see him until we went into the dining room for dinner.

As he came to the head of the table, he said: "My good people, we will serve ourselves as best we can with the cook's aid. We have no waitress to-night. But it is our last dinner. A camp under marching orders cannot fuss over trifles."

"Where is Angele?" asked the Divorcee. "Is she ill?" And she turned to the door.

"Come back!" said the Doctor, sharply. "You can't help her now. Better leave her alone!"

As if by instinct, we all knew what had happened.

"Who brought the news?" some one asked.

"They gave it to me at the *Mairie* as I passed," replied the Doctor, "and the *garde champetre* told me what the envelope contained. He fell at Charleroi."

"Poor Angele," exclaimed the Trained Nurse. "Are you sure I could not help her?"

"Sure," said the Doctor. "She took it as a Frenchwoman should. She snatched the baby from its cradle, and held it a moment close to her face. Then she lifted it above her head in both hands, and said, almost without a choke in her throat, *'Vive la France, quand meme!'*--and dropped. I put them on the bed together, she and the boy. She was crying like a good one when I left her. She's all right."

"Poor child--and that tiny baby!" exclaimed the Divorcee, wiping her eyes.

"Fudge," said the Doctor. "She is the widow of a hero, and the mother of the hero's son. Considering what life is, that is to be one of the elect of Fate. She'll go through life with a halo round her head, and, like most of the French women I have seen, she'll wear it like a crown. It becomes us, in the same spirit, to partake of the food before us. This life is a wonderful spectacle. If you saw an episode like that in a drama, at the theatre, you would all cheer like mad."

We knew he was right.

But the Youngster could not help adding, "That's twice--two days running, that the Doctor has told a story out of his turn, and both times he outraged the consign, for both times it was a war story."

That seemed to break the ice. We talked more or less war during dinner, but this time there were no disputes. Still I think we were glad when the cook trotted in with the trays, and with our elbows on the table, we turned toward the Violinist, who leaned against the high back of his chair, and with his long white hands resting on the carved arms, and his eyes on the ceiling--an attitude that he did not change during the narrative, began:

*　　*　　*　　*　　*

It was in the early eighties that I returned from Germany to my native land, and settled myself and my violin in the city of my birth.

I was not rich as my countrymen judge wealth, but, in my own estimation, I was well to do. I had enough to live without labor, and was, therefore, able to devote myself to my art without considering too closely the recompense.

In addition to that, I was still young.

I had more love for my chosen mistress--Music--than the Goddess had for me, for, while she accepted my worship with indulgence, she wasted fewer gifts on me than fell to the lot of many a less faithful follower.

Still, I was happy and content in my love for her, and only needed her to keep me so until, a year after my return, I met one woman, loved her, and begged her to share with my music, my heart, and its adoration.

That satisfied her, since, in her own love for the same art, she used to assure me that she possessed, by proxy, that other half of myself which I still dedicated to the Muse.

Perhaps it was the vibrant spirit of this woman which seemed musical to me, and which I so ardently loved, for she appeared to have a veritable violin soul. Her face was often the medium through which I saw the spirit of the music I was playing, as it sang in gladness, sobbed in sadness, thrilled in passion along the strings of my Amati.

I knew that I never played so well as when her face was before me. I felt that if ever I approached my dreams in achievement, it would be her soul that inspired me. So like was she, in my fancy, to a musical instrument, that I used to tell her, when the wind swept across her burnished hair, that the air was full of melody. And when she looked especially ethereal--as she did at times--I would catch her in my arms, and bid her tell me, on peril of her life, what song was hidden in her heart, that I might teach it to my violin, and die great. Yet, remarkable as it seems to me still, the Spirit of Music that surely dwelt within her, dwelt there a dumb prisoner. It had no audible voice, though I was not alone in feeling its presence in her eyes, on her lips, in her spiritual charm.

She had a voice that was melody itself, yet she never sang. I always fancied her hands were a musician's hands, yet she never played. This was the more singular as her mother had been a great singer, and her father, while he had never risen above the desk of *chef d'orchestre* in a local playhouse, was no mean musician.

Often, when the charm of her spirit was on me, I would pretend to weave a spell about her, and conjure the spirit that was imprisoned in the heart that was mine, to come forth from the shrine he was so impudently usurping.

Ah, those were the days of my youth!

We had been betrothed but a brief time when Rodriguez, for some seasons a European celebrity, made his first appearance in our city.

I had heard most of the great violinists of that time, had known some of them well, had played with many of them, as I did later with Rodriguez, but I had never chanced to see or hear him.

His fame had, however, preceded him. The newspapers were full of him. Faster even than the tales of his genius had travelled the tales of his follies--tales that out-Don-Juaned the famous rake of tradition.

However little credence one gives to such reports--mad stories of a scandalous nature--these repeated episodes of excesses, only tolerated in the conspicuous, do color one's expectations. I suppose that, being young, I expected to see a man whose face would bear the brand of his errors as well as the stamp of his genius.

That was not Rodriguez's fate. Whatever the temperamental struggle had been, he was "take him for all in all," the least disappointing famous man that my experience had ever shown me. He was more virile than handsome, and no more aesthetic to look at than he was ascetic. At that time he was on the sunny side of forty, and not yet at the zenith of his great career. His face was fine, manly, and sympathetic. His brow was broad, his eyes deep-set and widely spaced, but very heavy lidded. The mouth and chin were, I must own, too delicate and sensitive for the rest of the face. His dark hair, young as he was, had streaks of grey. In bearing he was so erect, so sufficient, that he seemed taller than he was. If he had the vanity which so often goes with his kind of temperament, it was most cleverly concealed. Safe in the dignified consciousness of his unquestioned gifts, secure in his achievements, he had a winning gentleness, and an engaging manner difficult to resist.

But for a singular magnetic light in his eyes, which belied the calm of his bearing, when he chanced to raise the heavy lids full on one--they usually drooped a little--but for a sensitive quiver along the too full lips, as if they still trembled from the caress of genius--the royal accolade of greatness--he might have looked to me, as he did to many, more the diplomat than the artist.

It would be useless for me to analyse his command of his instrument. I could not. It would be superfluous for me to recount his triumphs. They are too recent to have been forgotten. Both tasks have, moreover, been done better than I could do either.

This I can do, however, bear witness to the glowing wings of hope, of longing, of aspiration which his singing violin lent to hearts oppressed by commonplace every-day cares, to the moments of courage, of re-awakened endeavor which he inspired in his fellowmen, to the marvellous magnetism of his playing which seemed for the moment to restore to a soul-weary world its illusions, and to strike off the fetters of despondency which bind mortality to earth.

It was not alone the musically intelligent who felt this, for his playing had a universal appeal. Thorough musicians marvelled at and envied him his mastery of the details of his art, but it seemed to me that those who knew least of its technique were equally open to his influence.

I don't presume to explain this. I merely record it. There were those who analysed the fact, and explained it on the ground of animal magnetism. For myself, I only know that, as the magic music which Hunold Singref played in the streets of Hamelin, whispered in the ears of little children words of promise, of happiness, of comfort that none others could hear, so, to the emotional heart, Rodriguez's violin spoke a special message.

The man who sets the faces of the throng upward, and lights their eyes with the magic fire of hope, has surely not lived in vain, whatever personal offerings he may have made on the altar of his genius to keep alive the eternal spark. It cannot be denied that Art has fulfilled some part of its mission on earth, if, but for one hour, thousands, marshalled by its music, as the children of Israel by the pillar of flame, have looked above the dull atmosphere where pain and loss and sorrow are, to feel in themselves that divine longing which is ecstasy, that soaring of the spirit which, in casting off fear and rising above doubt, can cry out in joy, "Oh, blessed spark of Hope--this soul which can so rise above sorrow, so mount above the body, must be immortal. This which can so cast off care cannot die!"

All the great acts of life, and all the great arts, are purely emotional. I know that modern cults deny this, and work to see everything gauged by reason. But thus far musicians and painters, preachers and orators all approach their goal by the road to the emotions--if they hope to win the big world. Patriotism, fidelity--love of country, like love of woman--are emotions, and it would puzzle logicians, I am afraid, to be sure that these emotions, at times sublime, might not be as sensual as some of Rodriguez's critics found his music.

$$* \quad * \quad * \quad * \quad *$$

The series of concerts he gave was very exhausting to me, owing to the novelty of some of his programs, and the constant rehearsals. The final concert found me quite worn out.

During the latter part of the evening I had been too weary to even raise my eyes to the balcony in front of me, where, from my position among the first violins, I could see the fair face of my beloved.

The evening had been a great triumph, and when it was all over the audience was quite mad with enthusiasm. It was one of Rodriguez's inviolable rules to play a program exactly as announced, and never to add to it. In the month he had been in town, the public had learned how impossible it was to tempt him away from his rule. But Americans are persistent!

Again and again he had mounted the steps to the platform, and calmly bowed his thanks, while long drawn cheers surged through the noise of hand-clapping, as strains on the brass buoy up the melody. I lost count of the number of times he had ascended and descended the little flight of steps which led, behind a screen, from the artist's room to the stage, when, having turned in my seat to watch him, as he came up and bowed, and walked off again, I saw him, as he stood behind the screen, gazing directly over our heads, suddenly raise his violin to his ear and slowly draw the bow across the strings.

Almost before we could realize what had happened, he crossed the stage, stepped to his stand, and drew his bow downward.

The applause died sharply on the crest of a crescendo, and left the air trembling. There was a sudden hush. A few sank back in their seats, but most of them remained standing where they were, just as we behind him were suddenly fixed in our positions.

I have since heard a deal of argument as to the use and power of music as the voice of thought. I was not then--and I am not now--of that school which holds music to be a medium to transmit anything but musical ideas. So, of the effect of Rodriguez's music on my mind, or the possibility that, for some occult reason, I was for the moment **en rapport** with him, as after events forced me to believe, I shall enter into no discussion. I am merely going to record, to the best of my ability, my thoughts, as I remember them. I no more presume to explain why they came to me, than I do to analyse my trust in immortality.

As he drew his bow downward, as the first chord filled my ears, everything else faded away.

There was the merest prelude, and then the theme, which appeared, disappeared and re-appeared again and again to be woven about every emotion, at once developed and dominated me.

I seemed at first to hear its melody in the fresh morning air, where it soared upward above the gentle breezes, mingling in harmony with the matins of the birds and the softly rustling trees. Hopeful as youth, careless as the wind, it sang in gladness and in trust. Then I heard the same melody throb under the noonday glow of summer. Its tone was broadened and sweetened, but still brave and pure, when all else in Nature, save its clear voice, seemed sensuous. I saw gardens in a riot of color; felt love at its passionate consummation, ere the light seemed to fade slowly toward the sunset hour. The world was still pulsing with color, but the grey of twilight was slowly enwrapping it. Then the simple melody soared above the day's peacefullest hour, firm in promise on the hushed air. In the mystery of night which followed, when black clouds snuffed out the torches of heaven, when the silence had something of terror even for the brave, that same steadfast loving hopeful theme moved on, consoling as trust in immortality. Through youth to maturity, and on to age, it sang with the same reiterant, subduing, infallible loyalty--the crystallized melody of all that is spiritual in love, in adoration, in passion.

As it died away into the distance, as if its spirit, barely audible, were translated to the far off heavenly host, I strained my hearing to catch that "last fine sound" that passed so gently one "could not be quite sure where it and silence met," and for the first and last time in my life I had known all that a violin can do.

For a moment the hush was wonderful.

Rodriguez stood like a statue. His bow still touched the strings. Yet there was no sound that one could hear, though his own fine head was still bent, as though he, too, listened.

He gently dropped his bow--he smiled--we all came back to earth together.

Then such a scene followed as beggars description.

But he passed hurriedly out of sight, and no amount of tumult could induce him to even show himself again.

Slowly, reluctantly, the audience dispersed, still murmuring. The musicians picked up their traps, and wildly or soberly according to their temperaments, began to dispute. It was everywhere the same topic--the unknown work that Rodriguez had so marvellously played.

As for me--as he played, I seemed to be in the very heart of the melody, singing it too, as his violin sang it. As the song soared upward, my heart was filled with longing, with pain, with joy, with regret. As it gradually died into silence a mist seemed to pass from before my eyes, and I became suddenly conscious of the sweet face of my beloved, growing more and more distinct, until, as the last note died away, I was fully conscious that the music had passed between us, like a cloud, to obscure my sight utterly, and to recede as slowly, leaving her face before me.

I knew afterward, that, to all appearances, I had been gazing directly into her face all the time.

Through it all I had a vague sense that what he played was not new to me. It seemed like something I had long known and tried to say, but could not.

In a daze, I left the stage. Silently I put my violin in its case, pulled on my great coat, and turned up the collar about my face. I was sure I was haggard, and I did not wish her to remark it. I knew that I should find her waiting in the corridor with her father.

Just as I passed out of the artists' room, I was surprised to see Rodriguez standing there in conversation with her, and her father. He was, however, just leaving them, and did not see me.

I knew that her father had known him in Vienna, when the now great violinist was a mere lad, and I had heard that he forgot no one, so the sight gave me a merely momentary surprise.

As I joined her, and we stepped out into the night together, I could not help wondering if Rodriguez had noticed her sensitive violin face, as I tried to get a look into her eyes. I remembered afterward that, so wrapped was I in my own emotions, and so sure was I of her sympathy, that I neither noted nor asked how the music had affected her.

It was bitterly cold. We walked briskly, and parted at the door.

As I look back, I realize how much an egoist an emotional man can be, and in good faith be unconscious of it.

The day after the concert was Saturday--a day on which I rarely saw her, as it was my habit to spend all Sunday with her. I was always somewhat an epicure in my moral nature. I liked to pet my inclinations, as I have seen good livers whet their appetites, by self-denial.

All day I was restless and depressed.

At the piano, with my violin in my hand, it was still that same haunting melody that bewitched my fingers. Whatever I essayed led me, unconsciously, back to the same theme; and whenever that *motif* fell from my fingers her face appeared before my eyes so distinctly that I would have to dash my hand across them to wipe away the impression that it was the real face that was before me. Afterward, when I was calmer, I knew that this was nothing singular since, whether I had ever reflected on the fact or not, she was rarely from my mind.

As I played that melody over and over again, it puzzled me more and more. I could find nowhere within my memory anything that even reminded me of it. Yet I was vaguely familiar with it.

When evening came on I was more restless than ever. By nine o'clock I found it impossible to bear longer with my own company, and I started out. I had no destination. Something impelled me toward the Opera House, though I cared little for opera as a rule, that is, opera as we have it in America--fashionable and Philistine.

I entered the auditorium--the opera was "Faust"--just in season to hear the last half of the third act.

As the sensuous passionate music swelled in the sultry air of the dark garden at Nuremburg, I listened, moved by it as I always am--when I cannot see the over-dressed, lady-like Marguerite that goes a-starring in America. My eyes wandered restlessly over the audience. Suddenly there was a rushing, like the surging of waters, in my ears, which drowned the music, and I saw Rodriguez sitting carelessly in the front of a stage box. His eyes were fixed on me, and I thought there was an expression of relief in them.

Shocked that the unexpected sight of the man should have such an effect on me, I pulled myself together with an effort. The sound of the waters receded, the music rushed back, leaving me amazed at a condition in myself which should have rendered me so susceptible, in some subconscious way, to the undoubted magnetism of the man whose violin had so affected me the night before, and so haunted me all day, and in regard to whose composition I had an ill-defined, but insistent, theory which would intrude into my mind.

In vain I turned my eyes to the stage. I could not forget his presence. Every few minutes my glance, as if drawn by a magnet, would turn in his direction, and as often as that happened, whether he were leaning back to speak to some one hidden by the curtain, or watching the house, or listening intently to the music, I never failed to find that his eyes met mine.

I sat through the next act in this condition. Then I could stand it no longer. I felt that I might end by making myself objectionable, and that, after all, it was far wiser to be safe at home, than sitting in the theatre where I occupied myself in staring at but one person.

I made my way slowly up the aisle and into the foyer, and had nearly reached the outer lobby, when I suddenly felt sure that he was near.

I looked up!

Yes, there he was, and he was looking me directly in the face again. An odd smile came into his eyes. He nodded to me as he approached, and, with a quaint shake of the head, said: "I just made a wager with myself. I bet that if I encountered you in the lobby, without actually seeking you, and you saw me, I'd speak to you--and ask a favor of you. I am going to win that wager."

He did not seem to expect me to answer him. He simply turned beside me, thrust his arm carelessly through mine, and moved with me toward the exit.

"Let us step outside a moment," he said. It was easy to understand why. The hero of the night before could not hope to pass unnoted.

He stepped into the street.

It was a moonlit night. I remember that distinctly.

He lighted his cigarette, and held his case toward me. I shook my head. I had no desire to smoke.

We walked a few steps together in silence before he said: "I am trying to frame a most unusual request so that it may not seem too fantastic to you. It is more difficult than writing a fugue. The truth is--I have gotten myself into a bit of a fix--and I want to guard against its turning into something worse than that. I need some man's assistance to extricate myself."

I probably looked alarmed. Those forebears of mine will intrude when I am taken by surprise. He saw it, and said, quickly: "It is nothing that a man, willing to be of service to me, need balk at; nothing, in fact, that a chivalrous man would not be glad to do. You may not think very well of me afterward, but be sure you will never regret the act. I was in sore need of a friend. There was none at hand--if such as I ever have friends. Suddenly I saw you. I remembered your violin as I heard it behind me last night--an Amati, I fancy?"

I nodded assent.

"A beautiful instrument. I may some day ask you to let me try it--you and I can never be quite strangers after to-night."

He paused, pounded the side-walk with his stick, impatiently, as if the long preamble made him as nervous as it did me. Then, looking me in the face, he said rapidly: "This is it. When I leave the box, after the next act, do you follow me. Stay by me, no matter what happens. Stick to me, even though I ask you to leave me, so long as there is any one with me. Do more--stay by me, until, in your room or mine, you and I sit down together, and--well, I will explain what must, until then, seem either mad or ridiculous. Is that clear?"

I assured him that it was.

"Agreed then," he said.

By this time we were back at the door. The whole thing had not taken five minutes. We re-entered the theatre, and walked hurriedly through the lobby to the foyer. As we were about to separate, he laid a hand on either of my shoulders, and with a whimsical smile, said: "I'll dare swear I shall try to give you the slip."--The smile died on his lips. It never reached his eyes. "Don't let me do it. After the next act, then," and, with a wave of his hand, he disappeared.

I thought I was ridiculous enough when he had gone, and I realized that I had promised to follow this man, I did not know where, I did not know with whom, I did not know why.

It was useless for me to go back into the auditorium. I could not listen to the music. In spite of myself, I kept approaching the entrance opposite the box, and peering through the glass, like a detective. I knew I was afraid that he would keep his word and try to give me the slip. I never asked myself what difference it would make to me if he did. I simply took up the strange unexplained task he had given me as if to me it were a matter of life or death.

Even before the curtain fell, I had hurried round the house and placed myself with my back to the door, so that I could not miss him as he passed, and yet had no appearance of watching him. It was well that I did, for in an instant the door opened. He came out and passed me quickly, followed by a tall slender woman in a straight wrap that fell from her head to the ground, and the domino-like hood which completely concealed her face.

As he drew her hand through his arm, he looked back at me, over his shoulder. His eyes met mine. They seemed to say, "Is it you, old True-penny?" But he merely bent his head courteously and with his lips said, "Come!" I felt sure that he shrugged his shoulders resignedly, as he saw that I kept my word, and followed.

At the door he found his carriage. He assisted his companion in. Then in the gentlest manner he said in my ear, as he stood aside for me to enter, "In with you. My honor is saved, but repentance dogs its heels."

To the lady he said, "This is the friend whom you were kind enough to permit me to ask for supper."

She made no reply.

I uncovered my head to salute her, murmuring some vague phrase of thanks, which was, I am sure, inaudible. Then Rodriguez followed, and took his place beside me on the front seat.

As the door banged I could have sworn that the lady, whose face was concealed behind the falling lace of her hood, as if by a mask, spoke.

He thought so, too, for he leaned forward as if to catch the words. Evidently we were mistaken, for he received no response. He murmured an oath against the pavements and the noise, and turned a smiling face to me--and I? Why, I smiled back!

As we rattled over the pavings, through the lighted streets, no one spoke. The lady leaned back in her corner. Opposite her Rodriguez hummed "Salve! dimora" and I beside him, sat strangely confused and inert, still as if in a dream.

I had not even noted the direction we were taking, until I found that we had stopped in front of a French restaurant, one of the few Bohemian resorts the town boasted.

Rodriguez leaped out, assisted the lady, and I followed.

Just as we reached the top of the stairs, as I was about to follow them into one of the small supper rooms, like a flash, as if I were suddenly waking from a dream into conscious, with exactly the same sensation I have experienced many and many a morning when struggling back to life from sleep, I realized that the slender figure before me was as familiar as my own hand.

As the door closed behind us, I called her by name--and my voice startled even myself.

She threw back the hood of her cape and faced me.

Rodriguez had heard, too. He wheeled quickly toward us, as nearly broken from his self-control as a man so sure of himself could be.

Under the flash of our eyes the color surged up painfully in her pale face. There was much the same expression in our eyes, I fancy,--Rodriguez's and mine--but I felt that it was at his face she gazed.

I have never known how far it is given to woman to penetrate the mysteries of human nature, for she is gifted, it seems to me, with a dissimulation in which she wraps herself, as with an impenetrable veil of outward innocence, and ignorance, from our less acute perception and ruder knowledge.

There were speeches enough that it would have become a man in my position to make. I knew them all. But--I said nothing. Some instinct saved me; some vague fore-knowledge made me feel--I knew not why--that there was really nothing for me to say at that moment.

For fully a minute none of us moved.

Rodriguez recovered himself first. I cannot describe the peculiar expression of his eyes as he slowly turned them from her face to mine. So bound up was he in himself that I was confident that he did not yet suspect more than that she and I had met before. What was in her mind I dared not guess.

He composedly crossed to her. He gently unfastened her heavy wrap, carefully lifted it from her shoulders. He pushed a high backed chair toward her, and, with a smile, forced her to sit--she did look dangerously white. She sank into it, and wearily leaned her pretty head back, as if for support, and I noticed that her slender hands, as they grasped either arm of the chair, trembled, in spite of the grip she took to steady herself. I felt her whole body vibrate, as a violin vibrates for a moment after the bow leaves the strings.

"It is a strange chance that you two should know each other," he said, "and very well, too, if I may judge from your manner of addressing her?"

I moved to a place behind her chair, and laid my hand on it. "This lady is my affianced wife," I replied.

He did not change color. For an instant not a muscle moved. He did not stir a step from his place before the fire, where he stood, with his gaze fixed on her face. For one instant he turned his widely opened eyes on me--brief as the glance was, I felt it was critical. Then his lids quivered and drooped completely over his eyes, absolutely veiling the whole man, and, to my amazement, he laughed aloud.

But even as he did so, he spread his hands quickly toward us as if to apologize, and ghastly as the comment was, grotesque even, as it all seemed, I think we both understood. He hardly needed to say, "Pardon me," as he quickly recovered his strong hold on himself.

The next instant he was again standing erect before the fire, with his hands thrust deep into his pockets, and his voice was absolutely calm as he turned toward me and said, with a smile under his half lowered heavy lids, "I promised you, when I asked you to accompany me, that before we slept to-night I would explain my singular request. I hardly thought that I should have to do it, whether I would or not, under these circumstances. Indeed, it appears that you have the right to demand of me the explanation I so flippantly offered you an hour ago. I am bound to own that, had I dreamed that you knew this lady--that a relation so intimate existed between you--I should surely never have done of my own will this which Fate has presumed to do for me. What can I say to you two that will help or mend this--to you, my fellow musician, who were willing to stand my friend in need, without question; and to the woman you love, and to whom I owe an eternal debt--that we may have no doubts of one another in the future? I cannot make excuses well, even if I have the right to. I only hope we are all three so constituted that we may be able to feel that for a little we have been outside common causes and common results, and that you may listen to an explanation which may seem strange, pardon me, and part from me without resentment, being sure that I shall suffer, and yet be glad."

The face against the high-backed chair was very pale. She closed her eyes. His gaze was on her. He marked the change, I was sure. He thrust his hands still deeper into his pockets, as if to brace himself, and went on. "Last night her pure eyes looked into mine. I had seen her face before me night after night, never dreaming who she was. I had always played to her, and it had seemed to me at times as if the music I made was in her face. I could see nothing else. I seemed to be looking through her amber eyes, down, down into her deep beautiful soul, and my soul reached out toward her, with a sudden knowledge of what manhood might have been had all womanhood been pure; of what life might have been with one who could know no sin.

"It was only her face that I saw, as I stood waiting the end of the applause. I seemed to be gazing between her glorious eyes, as to tell the truth, I had more than once gazed in my dreams in the past month. I had already written the song that seeing her face had sung in my heart. It was with an irresistible longing, an impulse stronger than my will, to say to her just what her face had said to me,--though she might never know it was said to her--that I went back to the stage. Almost before I realized it, I was there. I felt the vibrant soul of my violin as I laid my cheek against it, and I saw the same spirit tremble behind the eyes of the fair face above me, as one sees a reflection tremble under the wind rippled water. The first chord throbbed on the air in response to it. Then I played what she had unconsciously inspired in me. It was in her eyes, where never swerving, immortal loyalty shone, that I read the deathless theme. Out of her nature came the inspiration. To her belongs the honor. I know--no one better, that as I played last night, I shall never play again; just as I realize that *what* I played last night my own nature could never of itself have created. It was she who spoke, it was not I. Let him who dares, try to explain that miracle."

She rose from her chair and moved toward him, and as she moved, she swayed pitifully.

He did not stir.

It was I who caught her as she stumbled, and I held her close in my arms. After a moment, she relaxed a little, and her head drooped wearily on my shoulder. He lowered his lids, and I felt that every nerve in his well controlled body quivered with resentment.

He motioned to entreat her to sit down again. She shook her head, and, when he went on, again, he for the first time addressed himself directly to her. "It was chance that set you across my path last night--you and your father. I recognized him at once. I knew your mother well. I can remember the day on which you were born, I was a lad then. Your mother was one of my idols. Why, child, I fiddled for you in your cradle. At the moment I realized who you were, you were so much a part of my music that you only appealed to me through that. But when I left you, I carried a consciousness of you with me that was more tangible. I had held your hand in mine. I feel it there still.

"I went directly to my room, alone. I sat down immediately to transcribe as much of what I had played as possible while it was fresh in my mind. As I wrote I was alone with you. But as the spirit of the music was imprisoned, I knew that you were becoming more and more a material presence to me. When I slept, it was to dream of you again--but, oh, the difference!

"I should have been grateful to you for the inspiration that you had been to me--and I was! But it had served its purpose. They tell me I never played like that before. I feel I never shall again. But the end of an emotion is never in the spirit with me.

"I started out this afternoon to find you, oblivious of the fact that I should have left town. I had the audacity to tell myself that I should be a cad if I departed without thanking the sweet daughter of your mother for her share in making me great. I had the presumption to believe in myself. It seemed natural enough to your good father that 'a whimsical genius,' as he called me, should be allowed the caprice of even tardily looking up his boyhood's acquaintance. He received me nobly, was proud that you should see I remembered him--and simply made no secret of it.

"Though I knew what you had seemed to me, I little realized that the child of true, fine musical spirits had a nature strung like my Strad--fine, clear, true, matchless, as well as inspiring. I spent a beautiful afternoon with you. I cannot better explain than by saying that to me it was like such a day as I have sometimes had with my violin. I call them my holy-days, and God knows I try to keep them holy,--though after too many of them follow a St. Michael and the Dragon tussle--and I mean no discredit to the Archangel, either.

"The honest old father, proud to trust his daughter to me,--in his kind heart he always considered me a most maligned man,--went off to the play and his Saturday night club. He told me that.

"We were alone together. It was then that I began to think that I could probably play on her nature as I did on my violin, and then, with a player's frenzy, to realize that I had been doing it from the first; that we had vibrated in harmony like two ends of a chord. Then I saw no more the spirit behind her eyes. I saw only the beautiful face in which the color came and went, the burnished hair so full of golden lights, on which I longed to lay my hand--the sensitive red lips--and the angel and the demon rose up within me, and looked one another in the face, and I heard the one fling the truth at the other, which even the devil no longer cared to deny--Ah, forgive me!--"

In his egoism of self-analysis and open confession, I am sure he did not realize how far he was going, until she buried her face in her hands.

Then he stepped across the room and stood before me as she rested her face in her hands against my breast.

"It was not especially clever--the last struggle against myself. I had never known such a woman before. I suppose if I had, I should have tortured her to death to strike new chords out of her nature,--and wept at my work! I had not the courage to tear myself abruptly away. I suggested an hour of the opera--I gave her the public as a protector--and they sang 'Faust.' It was then that, knowing myself so well, I looked out into the auditorium and saw you! It was Providence that put you in my way. I thought it was accident. I am sure I need say no more?"

I shook my head.

He leaned over her a moment. He gently took her hands from her face. Her eyelids trembled. For one brief moment she opened her eyes to his.

"You have given me one sweet day," he murmured. "Some part of your soul has called its music out of mine. That offspring of a miraculous sympathy will live immortal when all else of our two lives is forgotten. Remember to-day as a dream--and me as a shadow there--" he stopped abruptly. I felt her head fall forward. She had swooned.

Together we looked into the beautiful colorless face.

I loved music as I loved light. I was an artist myself. A great musician--and this man was one--was to me the greatest achievement of Art and Living.

I did not refuse the hand he held out. I buried mine in it.

I did not smile nor mistrust, nor misunderstand the tears in his eyes, nor despise him because I knew they would soon enough be dry. I did not doubt his sincerity when he said, "I have never done so bitter a thing as say 'good-bye' to this--though I know but too well such are not for me."

He bent over her, as if he would take her in his arms.

She was unconscious. I felt tempted to put her there. I knew I loved her as he could never love--yet I pitied him the more for that.

"Tell her," he whispered, "tell her, when she shall have forgotten this--as I hope she will--that for this hour at least I loved her; that losing her I am liable to love her long,--so we shall never meet again. I shall never cease to be grateful to the Providence that threw you in my way--after to-night. To-night I could curse it and my conscience with a right good will." With an effort he straightened himself. "You can afford to forgive me," he said, "for I--I envy you with all my heart."--And he was gone.

I heard his voice as he spoke to the waiter outside. I listened to his step as he descended the stairs. He had passed out of our life forever.

That was years ago.

She has long been dead.

He was not to blame if the sunshine that danced in music out of the eyes of the woman I loved never quite came back again. We were, all the same, happy together in our way. He was not to blame if it was written in the big book of Fate that it should be his heart, and not mine, that should read the song she bore in her soul.

Something must be sacrificed for Art. We sacrificed our first illusions--and the Song he read will sing on when even Rodriguez is but a tradition.

X

EPILOGUE
ADIEU
HOW WE WENT OUT OF THE GARDEN

The last word had hardly been uttered when the Youngster, who had been fidgeting, leaped to his feet.

"Hark!" he cried.

We all listened.

"Cannon," he yelled, and rushed out to the big gate, which he tore open, and dashed into the road.

There was no doubt of it. Off to the north we could all hear the dull far-off booming of artillery.

We followed into the garden.

The Youngster was in the middle of the road. As we joined him he bent toward the ground, as if, Indian-like, he could hear better. "Hush," he said in a whisper, as we all began to talk. "Hush! I hear horses."

There was a dead silence, and in it, we could hear the pounding of horses' hoofs in the valley.

"Better come in out of the rain," said the Doctor, and we obeyed. Once inside the gate the Doctor said, "Well, I reckon it is to-morrow at the latest for us. The truth of the matter is: I kept something from you this evening. The village was drummed out last night. As this road is being kept clear, no one passed here, and as we were ready to start at a moment's notice, I made up my mind to have one more evening. However, we've time enough. They can't advance to-night. Too wet. No moon. Come on into the house."

He closed and locked the big gate, but before we reached the house, there was a rush of horsemen in the road--then a halt--the Youngster opened the gate before it was called for. Two mounted men in Khaki rode in, stopped short at the sight of the group, saluted.

"Your house?" asked one, as he slid from his saddle and leaned against his horse.

"Mine," said the Doctor, stepping forward.

"You are not proposing to stay here?"

"No, we are leaving in the morning."

"Got any conveyances?"

"Two touring cars."

"Good. You don't mind my proposing that you go before daylight, do you?"

"Not a bit," replied the Doctor, "if it is necessary."

"That's for you to decide," said the other officer. "We are going to set up a battery in this garden. Awfully sorry, you know, but it can't be helped."

The Youngster, who had remained at the gate, came back, and whispered in my ear, "They are coming. It's the English still retreating. By Jove, it looks as if they would get to Paris!"

"How many are there of you?" asked the senior officer.

"Ten," replied the Doctor.

"Eleven," corrected the Divorcee. "I shall take Angele and the baby." And she started on a run for the garage.

"Perhaps," said the Doctor, looking through the open gate, where the weary soldiers were beginning to straggle by, "perhaps it will not be necessary for all of us to go." And he went close to the officers, and drew his papers from his pocket. There was a hurried whispered conversation, in which the Critic and the Journalist joined. When it was over, the Doctor said, "I understand," and returned to our group.

"Well, good friends," he said, "it really *is* farewell to the garden! The Critic and I are going to stay a bit. We are needed. The Youngster will drive one car, and the Lawyer the other. Get ready to start by three,--that will be just before daylight--

and get into the house, all of you. You are in the way here!"

Everybody obeyed.

We had less than three hours to get together necessary articles and all the time there was the steady marching of feet in the road, where what servants we had were standing with water and such small help as could be offered a tired army, and bringing in for first aid such of the exhausted men as could be braced up.

Long before we were ready, we heard the rumble of the artillery and the low commands of the officers. In spite of ourselves, we looked out to see the gray things being driven into the gate, and down toward the hillside.

"Oh," groaned the Divorcee, "right over the flower beds!"

"Bother it all, don't look out," shouted the Youngster from his room. "That's just like a woman! Be a sport!" And he dashed down the hall. We had just time to see that he had "put that uniform on." He was going into the big game, and he was dressed for the part. In a certain sense, all the men were, when we at last, bags in hand, gathered in the dining room, so we were not surprised to find the Nurse in her hospital rig, with a white cap covering her hair, and the red cross on her arm. We knew at once that she was remaining behind with the Doctor and the Critic.

The cars were at the door. Angele, with her baby in her arms, was sitting in one.

"Come on," said the Doctor, "the quicker you are out of this the better."

And, almost without a word, like soldiers under orders, we were packed into the two cars. The Youngster, the Lawyer, and the two officers stood together with their heads bent over a map.

"Better take a side road," said the officer, "until you get near to Meaux, then take the route de Senlis. It will lead you right over the hill into the Meaux, then you will find the *route nationale* free. Cross the Marne there, and on into Paris by the forest of Vincennes."

"Let the Lawyer lead," said the Doctor, "and be prudent, Youngster. You know where a letter will reach me. See that the girls get off safely!" He shook hands all round. The cars shot out of the gate, tooted for a passage through the straggling line of tired men in Khaki, took the first turn to get out of the way, and shot down the hill to the river.

"Well," said the Youngster, who was driving our car, with the Violinist beside him, "I think we behaved fine, and, by Jove, how I hate to go just now! But I have to join day after to-morrow, and I suppose it will be a long time before I see anything as exciting as this. Bother it. Well, you were amazed at the calmness only yesterday!"

No one replied. We were all busy with our own thoughts, and with "playing the game." In silence we crossed the first bridge. Day was just breaking as we mounted the hill on the other side. Suddenly the Youngster put on the brake.

"Here," he said to the Violinist, "take the wheel a moment. I must look back."

Just as he spoke there was a tremendous explosion.

"Bomb," he cried, as he got out his glass, and, standing on the running board, looked back. "They've got it," he yelled. "Look!"

We all piled out of the car, and ran to the edge of the hill. From there we could look back and just see the dear old house standing on the opposite height in its walled garden.

There was another explosion, and a puff of smoke seemed to rise right out of the middle of the garden, where the old tree stood, under which we had dined so many evenings.

For a few minutes we stood in silence.

It was the gentle voice of the Violinist that called us back. "Better get on," he said. "We can do nothing now but obey orders," and quietly we crawled back and the car started on.

We did not speak again until we ran up to the gates of Paris, and stopped to have our papers examined for the last time. Then I said, with a laugh: "And only think! I did not tell my story at all!"

"That's so," said the Youngster. "What a shame. Never mind, dear, you can tell the whole story!"--And I have.

The Codes Of Hammurabi And Moses
W. W. Davies

QTY

The discovery of the Hammurabi Code is one of the greatest achievements of archaeology, and is of paramount interest, not only to the student of the Bible, but also to all those interested in ancient history...

Religion   **ISBN: *1-59462-338-4***   **Pages:132**

MSRP $12.95

The Theory of Moral Sentiments
Adam Smith

QTY

This work from 1749. contains original theories of conscience amd moral judgment and it is the foundation for systemof morals.

Philosophy ISBN: *1-59462-777-0*   **Pages:536**

MSRP $19.95

Jessica's First Prayer
Hesba Stretton

QTY

In a screened and secluded corner of one of the many railway-bridges which span the streets of London there could be seen a few years ago, from five o'clock every morning until half past eight, a tidily set-out coffee-stall, consisting of a trestle and board, upon which stood two large tin cans, with a small fire of charcoal burning under each so as to keep the coffee boiling during the early hours of the morning when the work-people were thronging into the city on their way to their daily toil...

Pages:84

Childrens   ISBN: *1-59462-373-2*   *MSRP $9.95*

My Life and Work
Henry Ford

QTY

Henry Ford revolutionized the world with his implementation of mass production for the Model T automobile. Gain valuable business insight into his life and work with his own auto-biography... "We have only started on our development of our country we have not as yet, with all our talk of wonderful progress, done more than scratch the surface. The progress has been wonderful enough but..."

Pages:300

Biographies/   **ISBN: *1-59462-198-5***   *MSRP $21.95*

The Art of Cross-Examination
Francis Wellman

QTY

I presume it is the experience of every author, after his first book is published upon an important subject, to be almost overwhelmed with a wealth of ideas and illustrations which could readily have been included in his book, and which to his own mind, at least, seem to make a second edition inevitable. Such certainly was the case with me; and when the first edition had reached its sixth impression in five months, I rejoiced to learn that it seemed to my publishers that the book had met with a sufficiently favorable reception to justify a second and considerably enlarged edition. ..

Pages:412

Reference   ISBN: *1-59462-647-2*   *MSRP $19.95*

On the Duty of Civil Disobedience
Henry David Thoreau

QTY

Thoreau wrote his famous essay, On the Duty of Civil Disobedience, as a protest against an unjust but popular war and the immoral but popular institution of slave-owning. He did more than write—he declined to pay his taxes, and was hauled off to gaol in consequence. Who can say how much this refusal of his hastened the end of the war and of slavery ?

Law   ISBN: *1-59462-747-9*

Pages:48

MSRP $7.45

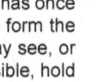

Dream Psychology Psychoanalysis for Beginners
Sigmund Freud

QTY

Sigmund Freud, born Sigismund Schlomo Freud (May 6, 1856 - September 23, 1939), was a Jewish-Austrian neurologist and psychiatrist who co-founded the psychoanalytic school of psychology. Freud is best known for his theories of the unconscious mind, especially involving the mechanism of repression; his redefinition of sexual desire as mobile and directed towards a wide variety of objects; and his therapeutic techniques, especially his understanding of transference in the therapeutic relationship and the presumed value of dreams as sources of insight into unconscious desires.

Pages:196

Psychology   ISBN: *1-59462-905-6*   *MSRP $15.45*

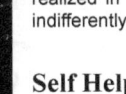

The Miracle of Right Thought
Orison Swett Marden

QTY

Believe with all of your heart that you will do what you were made to do. When the mind has once formed the habit of holding cheerful, happy, prosperous pictures, it will not be easy to form the opposite habit. It does not matter how improbable or how far away this realization may see, or how dark the prospects may be, if we visualize them as best we can, as vividly as possible, hold tenaciously to them and vigorously struggle to attain them, they will gradually become actualized, realized in the life. But a desire, a longing without endeavor, a yearning abandoned or held indifferently will vanish without realization.

Pages:360

Self Help   ISBN: *1-59462-644-8*   *MSRP $25.45*

www.bookjungle.com *email: sales@bookjungle.com fax: 630-214-0564 mail: Book Jungle PO Box 2226 Champaign, IL 61825*

QTY

The Rosicrucian Cosmo-Conception Mystic Christianity *by Max Heindel*   ISBN: *1-59462-188-8*   **$38.95**
The Rosicrucian Cosmo-conception is not dogmatic, neither does it appeal to any other authority than the reason of the student. It is: not controversial, but is: sent forth in the, hope that it may help to clear...   New Age/Religion Pages 646

Abandonment To Divine Providence *by Jean-Pierre de Caussade*   ISBN: *1-59462-228-0*   **$25.95**
"The Rev. Jean Pierre de Caussade was one of the most remarkable spiritual writers of the Society of Jesus in France in the 18th Century. His death took place at Toulouse in 1751. His works have gone through many editions and have been republished...   Inspirational/Religion Pages 400

Mental Chemistry *by Charles Haanel*   ISBN: *1-59462-192-6*   **$23.95**
Mental Chemistry allows the change of material conditions by combining and appropriately utilizing the power of the mind. Much like applied chemistry creates something new and unique out of careful combinations of chemicals the mastery of mental chemistry...   New Age Pages 354

The Letters of Robert Browning and Elizabeth Barret Barrett 1845-1846 vol II   ISBN: *1-59462-193-4*   **$35.95**
by Robert Browning and Elizabeth Barrett   Biographies Pages 596

Gleanings In Genesis (volume I) *by Arthur W. Pink*   ISBN: *1-59462-130-6*   **$27.45**
Appropriately has Genesis been termed "the seed plot of the Bible" for in it we have, in germ form, almost all of the great doctrines which are afterwards fully developed in the books of Scripture which follow...   Religion/Inspirational Pages 420

The Master Key *by L. W. de Laurence*   ISBN: *1-59462-001-6*   **$30.95**
In no branch of human knowledge has there been a more lively increase of the spirit of research during the past few years than in the study of Psychology, Concentration and Mental Discipline. The requests for authentic lessons in Thought Control, Mental Discipline and...   New Age/Business Pages 422

The Lesser Key Of Solomon Goetia *by L. W. de Laurence*   ISBN: *1-59462-092-X*   **$9.95**
This translation of the first book of the "Lernegton" which is now for the first time made accessible to students of Talismanic Magic was done, after careful collation and edition, from numerous Ancient Manuscripts in Hebrew, Latin, and French...   New Age/Occult Pages 92

Rubaiyat Of Omar Khayyam *by Edward Fitzgerald*   ISBN:*1-59462-332-5*   **$13.95**
Edward Fitzgerald, whom the world has already learned, in spite of his own efforts to remain within the shadow of anonymity, to look upon as one of the rarest poets of the century, was born at Bredfield, in Suffolk, on the 31st of March, 1809. He was the third son of John Purcell...   Music Pages 172

Ancient Law *by Henry Maine*   ISBN: *1-59462-128-4*   **$29.95**
The chief object of the following pages is to indicate some of the earliest ideas of mankind, as they are reflected in Ancient Law, and to point out the relation of those ideas to modern thought.   Religion/History Pages 452

Far-Away Stories *by William J. Locke*   ISBN: *1-59462-129-2*   **$19.45**
"Good wine needs no bush," but a collection of mixed vintages does. And this book is just such a collection. Some of the stories I do not want to remain buried for ever in the museum files of dead magazine-numbers an author's not unpardonable vanity..."   Fiction Pages 272

Life of David Crockett *by David Crockett*   ISBN: *1-59462-250-7*   **$27.45**
"Colonel David Crockett was one of the most remarkable men of the times in which he lived. Born in humble life, but gifted with a strong will, an indomitable courage, and unremitting perseverance...   Biographies/New Age Pages 424

Lip-Reading *by Edward Nitchie*   ISBN: *1-59462-206-X*   **$25.95**
Edward B. Nitchie, founder of the New York School for the Hard of Hearing, now the Nitchie School of Lip-Reading, Inc, wrote "LIP-READING Principles and Practice". The development and perfecting of this meritorious work on lip-reading was an undertaking...   How-to Pages 400

A Handbook of Suggestive Therapeutics, Applied Hypnotism, Psychic Science   ISBN: *1-59462-214-0*   **$24.95**
by Henry Munro   Health/New Age/Health/Self-help Pages 376

A Doll's House: and Two Other Plays *by Henrik Ibsen*   ISBN: *1-59462-112-8*   **$19.95**
Henrik Ibsen created this classic when in revolutionary 1848 Rome. Introducing some striking concepts in playwriting for the realist genre, this play has been studied the world over.   Fiction/Classics/Plays 308

The Light of Asia *by sir Edwin Arnold*   ISBN: *1-59462-204-3*   **$13.95**
In this poetic masterpiece, Edwin Arnold describes the life and teachings of Buddha. The man who was to become known as Buddha to the world was born as Prince Gautama of India but he rejected the worldly riches and abandoned the reigns of power when...   Religion/History/Biographies Pages 170

The Complete Works of Guy de Maupassant *by Guy de Maupassant*   ISBN: *1-59462-157-8*   **$16.95**
"For days and days, nights and nights, I had dreamed of that first kiss which was to consecrate our engagement, and I knew not on what spot I should put my lips..."   Fiction/Classics Pages 240

The Art of Cross-Examination *by Francis L. Wellman*   ISBN: *1-59462-309-0*   **$26.95**
Written by a renowned trial lawyer, Wellman imparts his experience and uses case studies to explain how to use psychology to extract desired information through questioning.   How-to/Science/Reference Pages 408

Answered or Unanswered? *by Louisa Vaughan*   ISBN: *1-59462-248-5*   **$10.95**
Miracles of Faith in China   Religion Pages 112

The Edinburgh Lectures on Mental Science (1909) *by Thomas*   ISBN: *1-59462-008-3*   **$11.95**
This book contains the substance of a course of lectures recently given by the writer in the Queen Street Hall, Edinburgh. Its purpose is to indicate the Natural Principles governing the relation between Mental Action and Material Conditions...   New Age/Psychology Pages 148

Ayesha *by H. Rider Haggard*   ISBN: *1-59462-301-5*   **$24.95**
Verily and indeed it is the unexpected that happens! Probably if there was one person upon the earth from whom the Editor of this, and of a certain previous history, did not expect to hear again...   Classics Pages 380

Ayala's Angel *by Anthony Trollope*   ISBN: *1-59462-352-X*   **$29.95**
The two girls were both pretty, but Lucy who was twenty-one who supposed to be simple and comparatively unattractive, whereas Ayala was credited, as her Bombwhat romantic name might show, with poetic charm and a taste for romance. Ayala when her father died was nineteen...   Fiction Pages 484

The American Commonwealth *by James Bryce*   ISBN: *1-59462-286-8*   **$34.45**
An interpretation of American democratic political theory. It examines political mechanics and society from the perspective of Scotsman James Bryce   Politics Pages 572

Stories of the Pilgrims *by Margaret P. Pumphrey*   ISBN: *1-59462-116-0*   **$17.95**
This book explores pilgrims religious oppression in England as well as their escape to Holland and eventual crossing to America on the Mayflower, and their early days in New England...   History Pages 268

www.ingramcontent.com/pod-product-compliance
Lightning Source LLC
Chambersburg PA
CBHW080735250626
47170CB00010B/2842